ORCA
YOUNG
READER

Ten Thumb Sam

RACHEL DUNSTAN MULLER

ORCA BOOK PUBLISHERS

Library and Archives Canada Cataloguing in Publication

Muller, Rachel Dunstan, 1970-
Ten Thumb Sam / written by Rachel Dunstan Muller.

(Orca young readers)
ISBN 978-1-55143-699-9

I. Title. II. Series.

PS8626.U4415T45 2007   jC813'.6   C2007-903850-6

First published in the United States, 2007
Library of Congress Control Number: 2007930414

Summary: Sam wants to run away from the circus because, unlike the rest of his family, he is "all thumbs."

Orca Book Publishers gratefully acknowledges the support for its publishing programs provided by the following agencies: the Government of Canada through the Book Publishing Industry Development Program and the Canada Council for the Arts, and the Province of British Columbia through the BC Arts Council and the Book Publishing Tax Credit.

Typesetting by Teresa Bubela
Cover artwork by Cindy Revell
Author photo by Bern Muller

ORCA BOOK PUBLISHERS
PO Box 5626, STN. B
VICTORIA, BC CANADA
V8R 6S4

ORCA BOOK PUBLISHERS
PO Box 468
CUSTER, WA USA
98240-0468

www.orcabook.com
Printed and bound in Canada.

10 09 08 07 • 4 3 2 1

For Rebecca, Naomi and Emily,
the original Stringbinis,
and for Anastasia, the new kid in the troupe.

Acknowledgments

Sam and his family were launched into the world with support and encouragement from the following people: my husband, Bernard Muller; my editor, Sarah Harvey; and the members of the Ballycastle Writer's Group. Thank you all!

Chapter One

Sam put his foot on the bottom rung of the long wire ladder and looked up. "I can do this," he whispered.

"What's that?" his brother Andrew asked.

"Nothing," said Sam. He swallowed. From this distance the high wire looked like a long piece of dental floss.

"If you're not ready," said Andrew, "we can try again tomorrow."

"I'm ready." Sam took a deep breath and began to climb, painfully aware that his entire family was watching him.

"I'm right behind you," Andrew said.

Learning to walk the high wire had seemed like a good idea to Sam a few months ago. But back then the practice wire was just a few inches off the ground. Andrew had helped Sam take his first teetering steps.

1

Sam worked hard every day until he could make it across the practice wire without falling. He'd looked more like a toddler taking his first steps than a tight-rope walker, but Andrew had assured him he would get more confident with time.

Sam wasn't feeling confident now, even with a harness and a safety rope to save him if he fell. His arms and legs were trembling. The higher he climbed, the more his body shook. "Uh, Andrew?" he said as his head drew even with the small wooden platform at the top of the ladder.

"Yeah?"

"I'm stuck," said Sam, trying not to panic.

"What do you mean, you're stuck?" his brother asked.

"I mean I can't let go of the last rung. My hands won't budge."

"Take a deep breath," said Andrew. "You'll be fine."

"I don't think so," Sam said through clenched teeth.

"Don't worry," said Andrew. "Everyone's nervous their first time up here. Just whatever you do, don't look down."

Sam immediately looked down and saw his mother, his father, his brother Martin, and his sisters Elizabeth,

Louise and Annabel. They looked impossibly small. Sam felt his stomach heave. "I think I'm going to be sick."

"Wait—," said Andrew.

It was too late. Sam's breakfast was already on its way up—and down.

"Looks like Elizabeth and Louise got the worst of it," Andrew said as he helped Sam descend. He shook his head. "Wouldn't want to be in your shoes when the twins catch up with you!"

Back on firm ground, Sam made straight for the Stringbini family bus. There were six narrow beds tucked into the back of the converted school bus. Sam and his two older brothers slept in the three curtained-off beds on the bottom level, and his sisters slept in the three bunks on the top. It wasn't your typical domestic arrangement, but then the Stringbinis weren't your typical family.

Each member of the Stringbini family had an important role in the Triple Top Circus. Each member, that is, except Sam. Sam's father, Magic Max, was a magician who helped manage the small circus. Sam's mother, Irene, was famous for the daring trapeze act she performed with Elizabeth and Louise, Sam's fourteen-year-old twin sisters. Sixteen-year-old

Andrew was the star of the Triple Top high wire. Thirteen-year-old Martin juggled colorful balls and flaming rings while balancing on a unicycle. Even Annabel had a role. Sam's six-and-a-half-year-old sister was Magic Max's assistant. The crowds loved Annabel, although Sam could never quite figure out why. Maybe it was her dimples and her blond ringlets. And the fact that they never saw her stamp her feet or pout when she didn't get her way.

Sam was the only one who didn't have an act. He was clumsy, forever tripping, stumbling and bumping into things. Because he was "all thumbs," Louise and Elizabeth had nicknamed their youngest brother "Ten Thumb" Sam. He was six years old the first time he heard this nickname. He had been so angry, he almost cried.

"You're just going through an awkward stage, sweetie," Irene had assured her son. "You'll grow out of it."

"When?" Sam demanded.

"I don't know," said his mother. "Everyone is different. You'll just have to be patient."

Sam tried to be patient as he waited for weeks, then months, then years. But watching from the sidelines was boring. No one ever cheered for Sam. *He* was never greeted with thunderous applause.

"I'm ready to be in the circus too," Sam had finally insisted shortly after his tenth birthday.

"But you are in the circus," said Max. "You help collect tickets, you sell cotton candy…"

Sam shook his head. "It's not the same. I want to be in the show, like the rest of you."

Sam's parents exchanged glances. "Where do you want to start?" Irene asked.

"The high wire," said Sam.

So much for that, he thought now as he entered the Stringbini bus and slammed the door behind him. If only he'd known he was terrified of heights. All that practice, all that hard work—it had all been for nothing!

Chapter Two

"You're up early," his father said as Sam stumbled out into the kitchen the next morning. Max was seated at the kitchen table. There was an empty porridge bowl in front of him and a mug of coffee in his hand. "How's your stomach feeling?" he asked.

"Okay," said Sam.

"Good. Then grab a bowl and fill it up. We've got our work cut out for us today."

The gray lumpy mass in the porridge pot did nothing to improve Sam's mood. He stared at it gloomily for a moment before lifting the ladle to serve himself. The porridge made a squelching noise as it landed in his bowl. With a sigh, Sam sat down beside his father.

The Triple Top Circus visited a new town each week, but the routine was always the same. Today was Monday. On Monday mornings the circus performers took down the high wire, dismantled the trapezes and packed away the tents. By lunchtime the Fritzi sisters' horses—the only large animals in the Triple Top—were in their trailers. By afternoon the circus was miles down the road.

They continued driving on Tuesday. On Wednesday they reached their destination and began setting up for their opening night on Thursday evening. There was a second show on Friday night, two more on Saturday and a final matinee performance on Sunday. A week from now the cycle would begin all over again. It was always the same.

As Sam picked at his porridge, his brothers and sisters began to emerge from the back of the bus. He tried to ignore them as they served themselves and settled noisily around him at the table, but it was impossible.

"If I sit here, you're not going to barf on me, are you?" Annabel demanded as she took the chair beside Sam.

"Oh, be quiet," said Sam.

"Just checking."

"Leave your brother alone," Max said as he rose from the table. "He's got a lot to think about."

"Like what?" said Louise.

"Like what he's going to do next, right, Sam? The high wire didn't work, so he's going to find something else. No room for quitters in the Stringbini family."

"Don't even *think* about the trapeze," Elizabeth warned.

"You might want to try something a little closer to the ground," Andrew suggested.

Sam felt his face grow warm. "Maybe I could try juggling with Martin."

Sam's middle brother shrugged. "Sure, whatever. I could teach you a few things."

Sam had his first juggling lesson later that afternoon, once the circus trailers were loaded. He listened carefully to his brother's directions, but no matter how hard he tried, he couldn't seem to keep more than one ball in the air at a time.

"Loosen up," said Martin. "Relax. It's just throw and catch, throw and catch. You've got to find your rhythm."

"I don't *have* any rhythm," Sam protested.

"Keep practicing," said Martin. "You'll get it eventually."

Sam practiced for weeks with everything he could get his hands on: tennis balls, rubber balls, beanbags, even bars of soap. At night he dreamt of golden balls spinning high above him in a shining arc. But when he woke up he was still Ten Thumb Sam.

"All right, enough already," Martin said as he dodged a wayward beanbag one afternoon. "You're hopeless at this!"

"But I'm still learning," Sam protested.

"Learning what, exactly? You *still* can't keep more than one thing in the air at a time. But, hey," Martin shrugged, "you tried."

Sam crossed juggling off his list and went to see his cousin Tony Zuccato. He found him practicing his tumbling act with the other Zuccatos in the big top.

"What do you think?" Tony asked the others after Sam had explained the purpose of his visit. "Shall we give the kid a try?"

Tony's sister, Tina, grinned at Sam. "Why not?"

Sam was determined to get it right this time. He watched his cousins closely and listened carefully as they explained every move they made on the tumbling mat. But when it was his turn to tumble, he could barely manage a simple somersault, let alone a triple cartwheel or a flying leap.

"I'll get it," he promised through gritted teeth.

Sam threw himself into his new sport. He practiced every moment he could. When the Zuccatos were performing inside the big top, Sam was outside on the grass, attempting handstands and backflips. But for all his hard work, Sam just couldn't get his limbs to cooperate.

After being knocked flat for the seventeenth time in one morning while assisting his young cousin, Tony Zuccato had to speak up. "I'm really sorry, kid. You just don't have the moves."

"But I'll keep working!" Sam pleaded. He looked around at the rest of the Zuccato team. His cousin Harry had a bruise under one eye. Frankie's arm was in a sling. Only Tina, who was holding a block of ice to her knee, was able to meet Sam's gaze.

"Sorry, Sam," she said. "No hard feelings, but you're just too clumsy to be a tumbler."

Sam offered to help Mr. Poponopolis with his dog act.

"Don't see why not," Mr. Poponopolis said, scratching his bald head thoughtfully. "The dogs certainly seem to like you."

It was true that Mr. Poponopolis's dogs liked Sam,

especially when he scratched them behind their ears or stroked their bellies. But liking someone is one thing and obeying them is quite another. No matter what Sam ordered them to do, the terriers just wagged their short tails and stared up at him blankly. He tried begging them, pleading with them, bribing them with soup bones and doggie treats. In desperation he even got down on all fours and demonstrated the actions he wanted the dogs to perform. They didn't budge.

"I don't understand it," said Mr. Poponopolis. "I've never seen anything like it. Roll over," he said to the nearest dog. The dog rolled over.

"Roll over," said Sam. The dog stayed put.

Mr. Poponopolis shrugged his shoulders. "Sorry, Sam."

The Fritzi sisters were grooming their champion stallions when Sam approached them and asked if he could work with the horses.

"I don't know," said Erma Fritzi, biting her lip. "They're high-spirited animals. They can be very dangerous. They're not ponies, you know."

Imelda Fritzi rubbed her skinny hands together anxiously. "Are you sure it's all right with your parents?"

"I'm sure," said Sam.

"I don't know," Erma repeated.

"It's not that we don't trust you," said Imelda.

"We do, of course—"

"Trust you, that is—"

"It's just that it's so risky, working with large animals—"

"Please," said Sam. "I'll be careful."

The two sisters exchanged nervous glances. "Well, if you have your heart set on it," Erma said reluctantly.

"Of course," said Imelda, "we'd have to let them get used to you slowly. You could start by cleaning out the horses' trailers every day."

"Then I suppose we could teach you to groom them," said Erma.

Sam nodded. "I can do that."

"Are you sure?" Erma asked. "It's not glamorous work, believe me."

"We'd understand if you changed your mind," Imelda added.

"I'm sure," said Sam. "I won't change my mind."

"You're very determined, aren't you?" Erma said with a sigh. "All right then. If the horses get comfortable with you, we'll see about getting you into the saddle. Then we'll go from there."

But the Fritzi stallions never did get comfortable with Sam. His clumsiness made the horses nervous. They whinnied and shied away whenever he was near them. Once again, Sam was forced to admit defeat.

Chapter Three

A few days after Sam called it quits with the Fritzi stallions, Max found Sam sitting alone under one of the bleachers in the big top.

"How's it going?" Max asked, crouching down beside his son.

"Lousy," said Sam. "I don't fit in anywhere. I can't do anything."

Max put his hand on Sam's shoulder. "C'mon. You're not giving up already, are you?"

"Already?" said Sam. "I've tried everything! It's hopeless."

"You haven't tried everything. Have you talked to the clowns yet? You'd be a natural with them."

"Thanks a lot."

"But why not?" asked Max. "If you tripped over your feet, the audience would think it was part of the act."

Sam shook his head. "I don't want to be a clown! I don't want people laughing at me. I want them to clap and cheer the way they do for you!"

Sam's father was quiet for a few seconds. "Well, you know I already have an assistant—"

"You don't have to say anything," Sam interrupted, looking down at his feet. "I understand. I'd just mess up your act anyway."

"Now wait a minute," his father said, holding up a hand. "As I was saying, I already have an assistant. What I don't have is an apprentice."

Sam looked up. "An apprentice?"

Max nodded. "Every great magician should have an apprentice, don't you think?"

"You mean it? You're really serious?" A grin spread slowly across Sam's face. "Thanks, Dad. I won't let you down!"

On a bright Monday morning in early June, Sam's mother took the wheel of the Stringbini bus. Ten minutes later, the entire convoy of packed circus vehicles was on the highway.

"Ready, Sam?" Max asked from his place at the head of the kitchen table.

Sam was seated a few chairs down. He nodded. "Ready."

"Ahem," said Max. "I have an announcement to make. As you know, Sam and I have been working together on a magic act for the last little while. Sam has worked hard, and we both believe he's ready for his first performance."

"Way to go, Sam," Andrew said, tapping his fist against his brother's shoulder.

"Your hands are shaking," said Annabel.

Sam put his hands under the table and glared at his little sister.

"Annabel," Irene called from the driver's seat. "Be nice!"

When his sisters and brothers were seated around the table, Sam wiped his damp palms on his pants and stood up. He took a deep breath and then demonstrated each of the simple scarf tricks that his father had taught him. When the last scarf had disappeared, the assembled Stringbinis clapped politely.

"Good one, Sammy," Martin said.

"That wasn't half bad," said Louise.

"I know where the scarves went," said Annabel.

"Shhh, Annabel!" said Elizabeth.

"I told you you could do it, Sam," Max said. "Well done!"

Sam performed again that evening for the remaining members of the circus. He was nervous, but somehow he made it right through to the last trick without messing anything up.

"Congratulations!" Mr. Pigatto, the ringmaster, said while Sam was wiping his forehead in relief. "What do you say, Sam? Think you're ready for the big top?"

Sam swallowed. "I think so."

Max clapped a hand on Sam's shoulder. "We'll have to spend a little more time fine-tuning Sam's act. Then I know he'll be ready."

"Thanks again, Dad," Sam told his father before going to bed that night.

"My pleasure," said Max. "I'm proud of you for working so hard."

For the first time in many months, Sam went to sleep with a smile on his face.

Chapter Four

The Triple Top Circus was set up on the edge of a small prairie town when Sam's big night finally arrived. Bright lights lit up the sky, and lively music boomed from every loudspeaker. Eager crowds streamed into the big top, jostling good-naturedly for the best seats.

Irene stood waiting with Elizabeth and Louise in the small performers' tent that opened into the big top. Their trapeze act would open the night's show. Sam sat in a folding chair beside them, fidgeting nervously.

"Are you all right, sweetie?" Irene asked.

"I'm fine," Sam lied.

Louise looked up from the fingernail she was filing. "He looks kind of green."

Elizabeth nodded knowingly. "At least *this* time we won't be beneath him when he tosses his cookies."

"Girls," said Irene, "leave your brother alone." She turned back to Sam. "*Are* you feeling sick?"

Sam shook his head.

"You sure?"

He nodded.

"All right then," said his mother. "There's Mr. Pigatto announcing our act—we've got to go." She planted a big kiss on Sam's forehead before moving to the entrance of the main tent. "You're going to be great, sweetie."

Sam let himself slump forward when he was alone. He was *not* fine, but he wasn't going to admit it with the twins standing nearby. His hands were damp and trembling. The loud music and bright lights of the neighboring tent were giving him a headache. He'd already lost his dinner in the privacy of a toilet stall, but he still felt queasy. And if he felt like this here in the shadows, he had no idea how he was going to survive ten minutes in the spotlight.

"Ready, Sam?" Max asked as he slipped in to stand beside Sam's folding chair.

"Sure," Sam said with a forced smile.

"What about you, Annabel?"

Annabel's blond ringlets bobbed up and down. "I'm always ready, Daddy."

Sam watched from the doorway of the performers' tent as his mother appeared in the center ring of the big top with Elizabeth and Louise by her side. One by one, the three Stringbini women climbed up the ladder to the trapeze platform and began their flying act. Spotlights followed each swing, each twist and turn, each spectacular leap. Their performance was flawless, as usual. The crowd "oohed" and "aahed" and gave them a standing ovation when they were done.

Mr. Poponopolis's dogs followed the trapeze act. Then it was time for the Fritzi sisters and their stallions and a comic performance by the Triple Top clowns. There was a brief noisy intermission before Mr. Pigatto, the ringmaster, called everyone back. Sam's brother Andrew appeared next, high above the center ring on the high wire. When the audience finished cheering at the end of Andrew's act, it was Martin's turn to do figure eights on his unicycle while juggling a set of cups and saucers.

Sam had watched his family perform a thousand times, but tonight was different. Tonight he was finally going to prove that he belonged and that he could perform in front of an audience as well as any of his family members. "Oh please, *please* let me get through this without messing up," Sam whispered.

All too soon, the stout ringmaster was giving the magicians their cue. "And NOW, LADIES and GENTLEMEN," Mr. Pigatto cried. "Please turn your attention to the FAR RING to see the NEXT ASTOUNDING ACT. MAGIC MAX and his DARLING ASSISTANT ANNABEL will THRILL and AMAZE you. And TONIGHT, for the first time EVER, Magic Max will appear in public with his APPRENTICE, a young master of the magic arts, SLEIGHT-OF-HAND SAM!"

The crowd cheered as Max pushed Sam into the spotlight. It was a disaster from the start. The spectators waited for Sam to begin his first trick, but he was frozen to the spot.

"Sam!" said Annabel. She elbowed her brother in the ribs.

"It's okay, son," Max said quietly. "Take a deep breath. You'll be fine."

Sam rubbed his side and blinked.

"It's okay," Max repeated. "Just concentrate on your first trick." He tapped his sleeve as a reminder.

Sam swallowed and nodded. The first trick was a simple one that he'd already demonstrated several times for his family. It involved a string of brightly colored silk scarves that Sam would pull out of a secret

21

lining in his sleeve. He'd practiced it a hundred times, and it had always worked.

With trembling hands, Sam took off his jacket, turned it inside out and held it up for the audience's inspection. He put the jacket back on again.

"It's inside out," Annabel hissed through the smile pasted on her dimpled face.

"What?" Sam said blankly.

"Your jacket—it's still inside out!"

The audience laughed as Sam took off his jacket, turned it right side out and put it back on again.

"One potato, two potato," he said softly.

"Speak up!" Max whispered.

"Three potato, *blue* potato," Sam finished, only a fraction louder.

As the audience leaned forward in their seats to get a better view, Sam reached up his sleeve to pull out the string of scarves. The tip of a bright orange scarf emerged, but that was all. His face red, Sam tugged harder. A green scarf appeared. Sam strained to pull out the remaining scarves, but succeeded only in tearing off the green scarf. The crowd began to laugh and jeer.

"Ahem," said Mr. Pigatto, quickly stepping in to distract the audience. "If I may have your ATTENTION, MAGIC MAX is preparing his NEXT ILLUSION.

Watch closely and before your VERY EYES, Magic Max's lovely young assistant, ANNABEL, will enter the MYSTERIOUS WOODEN BOX and DISAPPEAR!"

Annabel quickly got into position inside the crate. Sam stumbled as he was trying to get out of the way, and at that moment the evening's events seemed to switch into slow motion. In an attempt to catch himself, Sam knocked over the cart that held his father's magic equipment. Everything went flying. Sam was soaked in colored water, a bouquet of flowers landed on his head, and an assortment of magic wands fell around his feet. As it fell, the cart caught the side of Annabel's box, and it too tipped over, breaking apart as it hit the ground.

Startled by the noise, Snowball, Max's white rabbit, hopped out from under an overturned top hat and bounded across the ground. Before anyone could stop him, the rabbit had escaped under one of the bleachers.

A cage of doves had also been knocked over. The distressed birds circled the audience several times before settling themselves on the high wire.

Max helped his youngest daughter out of the broken crate. Annabel's smile had disappeared. There was fury in her blue eyes.

For a moment the shocked crowd remained silent. Even Mr. Pigatto seemed at a loss for words. Then a few small children in the front row started giggling, and the silence was broken. Soon everyone in the big top was howling with laughter. Everyone, that is, but Sam.

Chapter Five

"Come on, Sam," his mother said, two weeks after his disastrous first performance. "It's your birthday. Everyone's waiting for you in the big top."

"Tell them I'm sick," Sam said from behind the curtain of his bunk bed.

Irene pushed the curtain aside. "You can't hide in here forever. Come on. Mrs. Pigatto made ham and pickle sandwiches."

"I'm not hungry," Sam insisted as his mother took his arm and began pulling him out.

"Not even for pistachio ice cream?" said Irene. "Oh well. More for your brothers, then."

"All right, I'm coming," Sam grumbled.

The circus performers cheered as Sam entered the tent behind his mother. When Sam was just a few yards away, Max waved a silk scarf in the air and a cake with eleven flickering candles appeared. Everyone clapped, even though they'd seen the trick a hundred times before. Sam waited until the performers had finished singing "Happy Birthday" before he blew out the candles.

"So what did you wish for?" Annabel demanded when the last candle was out.

"Don't you know if he tells you what he wished for, his wish won't come true?" Martin said.

"Yeah, silly," said Elizabeth.

"No," said Sam. He stood up straight. "It's all right. This time I want everyone to know what my wish is."

"That's the spirit," said Mr. Pigatto. "What did you wish for this year, Sam? A new bike?"

Sam screwed his eyes shut and blurted it out. "I'm tired of high wires and trapezes and magic acts. I'm tired of standing on the sidelines and living on a bus and traveling to a new town every week. I just want—"

Sam's speech was interrupted by a commotion outside the tent. "I just want to leave the circus," Sam finished quietly. But it was too late. He'd already lost his audience. Everyone had turned to watch the group of people that was spilling noisily through the entrance of the big top.

Sam immediately recognized the large, red-bearded man at the front of the group. It was his Uncle Albert, followed by the rest of Albert's family.

"You made it!" said Sam's mother. "Welcome!"

"Oh dear," said Sam's Aunt Mabel. "I do hope we aren't interrupting anything."

"Of course not, Mabel," Irene said graciously. "We were just celebrating Sam's birthday. There's enough cake here for everyone." Irene turned to face the rest of the Triple Top performers. "You remember I was telling you about my brother and his family?"

"Pleased to meet you," said Mr. Pigatto.

"Albert Horatio Goldfinger at your service." Albert gave a little bow. "And this is my wife, Mabel," he said, "and my sons, Herbert and Robert." Two tall, skinny, freckled boys with buzz cuts stepped forward. Sam barely recognized his redheaded cousins. They'd been about ten years old the last time he'd seen them. Now they were thirteen or fourteen.

"Call me Herbie," said the first, holding up his hand.

"Robbie," said the second.

"This is my oldest daughter, Mary Ann," Albert continued as a bored-looking teenager with curly red hair nodded vaguely in the group's direction. She hadn't changed as much as her brothers.

27

"And my youngest daughter, Harriet," Albert finished. Harriet nodded and smiled. She was Sam's age. She had freckles, like her brothers, but her hair was straight and brown rather than red. A magpie perched on her left shoulder.

"What's going on?" Sam whispered to his brother Andrew. "What are they doing here?"

"Shhh," said Andrew. "Mom's about to explain."

Irene cleared her throat. "As many of you know, my brother's family would ordinarily be touring the Maritimes right now with the Leaping Lizard Circus."

"It's a long and tragic story," Albert interrupted, "but our circus has fallen on hard times. We were all given our walking papers two weeks ago. The Lizard," he looked down at his shoes and shook his head sadly, "is no more."

There was a collective gasp, and then everyone started to talk at once. Mr. Poponopolis said something in Greek, while the Fritzi sisters and the Zuccatos slipped back into their native Italian.

"NOT the Leaping Lizard," Mr. Pigatto said, speaking for all of them. "The Leaping Lizard is a Canadian institution!"

Albert nodded. "Alas, it *was*. It would have celebrated its seventy-fifth anniversary this September."

"Oh, you poor dears," said Mrs. Pigatto as she patted Mabel's trembling hands. "Whatever are you going to do?"

"Until they get back on their feet, they're going to travel with us," said Irene. "After all, what's one more bus in our convoy?"

Albert cleared his throat. "Actually, I'm afraid we've had a bit of bad luck in that department as well. I had a few debts of my own. I couldn't cover them when the circus went bankrupt, so our bus was seized."

"Goodness," said Mrs. Pigatto, clutching her generous chest. "However did you get here?"

"We had just enough money to purchase bus tickets," said Albert.

"Then you'll have to move in with us for a little while," said Irene. "Don't you worry, Mabel," she said to her sister-in-law. "Everything will be fine."

In the excitement of welcoming the new family to the Triple Top, everyone had forgotten Sam and his birthday. Sam watched as his brothers and sisters followed the Goldfingers outside to help them gather up their belongings.

"They're all staying with us?" he asked his father. "In our bus?"

Max shrugged his shoulders. "Looks like it."

"But how are they all going to fit?"

"I'm not exactly sure," said Max. "The bus is small enough with eight of us crammed in."

"We'll make it work, Max," Sam's mother said as she came up beside them. "Albert and Mabel can have our sleeping compartment, and you and I can sleep on the kitchen benches. Elizabeth and Louise can squeeze in together to free up a bunk for Mary Ann, and Harriet can bunk with Annabel. That leaves Herbie and Robbie. They can sleep in Sam's bunk."

"What about me?" said Sam.

"You'll have to sleep on the floor for now."

"But why can't some of them sleep on the other buses?" Sam asked. "Why do they all have to crowd in with us?"

Irene sighed. "They've been through enough already without being separated as well. Besides, these are your cousins we're talking about. They're family. It's our responsibility to make room for them."

"Is that a *cat* Mary Ann's got in that crate?" Sam's father said as the Goldfingers re-entered the big top.

"They have two cats, if I remember correctly," said Irene. "Siamese. And a chameleon and a magpie."

"Do we have to share our bus with the animals too?" asked Sam.

Max looked over at his wife, one eyebrow raised.

"No, we're not going to share the bus with the animals," Irene said. "And please try to remember—both of you—this is only temporary."

Chapter Six

"There's only one way to do this," Sam's mother announced as ten cranky kids stumbled out of the back sleeping area looking for breakfast the next morning. "Some of you will have to eat outside. How about boys outside today, girls outside tomorrow?"

The boys grumbled as they received their bowls of porridge and made their way outside to the picnic table next to the bus. The girls didn't sound much happier inside. Through an open window, Sam heard his sisters complain about the cramped sleeping arrangements, while Mary Ann expressed her displeasure at being forced to eat porridge for breakfast.

"Hey, watch it!" Sam said angrily as Martin bumped against him. "You made me spill half my oatmeal!"

Martin shrugged. "It's not my fault your shoulder was in the way of my elbow. Watch where you sit next time."

Sam was still in a bad mood later that morning when he passed his cousin, Harriet, seated in the shade of one of the trailers. He was going to keep walking, but she lowered the book she was reading and called out to him.

"Hey," she said. "Why aren't you getting ready for this afternoon's show like everyone else?"

Sam scowled. "I suppose they told you everything."

"What do you mean?"

"Oh c'mon! The rabbit, the doves, the way the stupid audience laughed!"

Harriet looked blank. "I don't know what you're talking about. No one's said anything to me about anything."

Sam stared at his cousin suspiciously for a moment. "Seriously?"

"I swear."

"Okay, I believe you," Sam said as he sat down. "So what's with the bird?" he asked, pointing to the magpie on Harriet's shoulder. "Is he part of your act?"

"Loki? No, he's just a pet. I found him when he was a baby. His nest fell out of a tree near where our circus was set up, and I rescued him. I don't have an act."

"Really?" said Sam. "I thought I was the only circus kid without any talent."

"I have talent," said Harriet. "I'm good at lots of things. I've been reading since I was three, and I play chess online whenever I can get an Internet connection. No one in my family will play with me anymore. They're tired of getting slaughtered."

Sam shook his head. "Not that kind of talent— I mean like juggling, or walking the tightrope. That's what counts in a circus. C'mon, you must feel left out sometimes."

Harriet shrugged. "I don't know. Not really. My mother always says that there's more to life than the circus. She never wanted to be a performer herself. She's too shy. But she was born into a circus family, and then she married my dad and became his assistant in his magic act. So she's kind of stuck."

"I'm the only one who feels stuck in my family," said Sam. "I'd give anything to be with ordinary people for a change."

The Stringbini bus was in an uproar when Sam walked back at lunchtime.

"I don't eat animals," Mary Ann said as she refused

a bologna sandwich that Sam's mother was trying to give her.

"If she doesn't have to, then I don't either," said Louise, crossing her arms.

"I *hate* egg salad," Annabel pouted.

Herbie and Robbie spoke in unison: "We're allergic to peanut butter."

"And by the way," said Robbie, "has anyone seen Oliver?"

"Who's Oliver?" Sam asked.

"Our pet chameleon," said Herbie. "He's escaped from his terrarium."

The commotion was too much for Aunt Mabel. She looked as if she was about to cry.

Sam's mother took control. "Okay, listen up everybody," said Irene. "The bologna sandwiches go to the boys. Annabel and Mary Ann, you can have peanut butter and jam. Louise and Elizabeth, take the egg salad sandwiches. And if anyone's still not happy, they can wait until the bus clears out and make their own lunch with whatever's left. Good luck to you."

While the two mothers were doing their best to get lunch under control in the kitchen, Sam could hear his father having an intense discussion with his uncle at the front of the bus.

"It's really not necessary," Sam heard his father say.

"But I insist," replied Albert. "We intend to pay our own way."

"But you've only just arrived," said Max. "You need time to rest!"

"Nonsense," said Albert. "We're all perfectly rested, thanks to your hospitality."

"Well then, at least give yourselves time to see how we do things, if nothing else," Max argued. "Then we'll figure out how to introduce your acts into the Triple Top show."

"It's simple," said Albert. "We'll perform our acts in the order you do them, one after another: Triple Top, Goldfingers, Triple Top, Goldfingers. We'll start at tomorrow's matinee."

"But Albert," said Max, "why would we want two magic acts, one after another?"

"We'll be giving the audience good value—twice the show for the same price!"

Max's voice began to rise. "But we'd be out there all day and all night if we did that!"

"Not at all," said Sam's uncle. "We'll shave a little time off our acts, and you can shave a little time off yours. It will be fabulous!"

The discussion continued, but Sam had had enough of the noise and confusion. He grabbed his bologna sandwich and a handful of carrot sticks and headed back outside.

Chapter Seven

"There you are," said Harriet.

It was Saturday afternoon, and Sam was sitting at the picnic table outside the Stringbini bus, playing *Lightning Smash Blasters* on Martin's Pocket-Nitro.

The magpie on Harriet's shoulder flapped its wings as she sat down beside Sam. "The show's going to start in fifteen minutes," Harriet said. "Want to watch with me?"

Sam remained focused on his game. "Why? It's always the same."

"I've never seen your family perform before. And you've never seen mine, either," Harriet pointed out. She lifted Loki from her shoulder and put him inside the birdcage tucked in the shade of the bus.

"I'm sick of circus acts, all of them," said Sam.

"Suit yourself," Harriet said with a shrug.

She was halfway to the big top when Sam caught up with her.

"Changed my mind," he replied in response to his cousin's lifted eyebrow. "My batteries went dead. I've got nothing better to do while I wait for them to recharge."

"Your ringmaster looks like he's about to have a heart attack," Harriet said as she and Sam munched on caramel corn during intermission.

Mr. Pigatto did look a little more excited than usual. He was waving his hands in the air as he addressed Sam's father and some of the other performers. He paused to wipe his forehead with a red handkerchief, and then he pointed dramatically at his left wrist.

Sam checked his own watch. "Mr. Pigatto has this thing about keeping everybody on time. I guess he's not happy about how long the show is running with all the extra acts."

"Look over there," said Harriet. She pointed across the tent to the performers' entrance. "Mary Ann is throwing one of her hissy fits. That will be about having to cut back her time on the high wire. If Mary Ann had her way, she'd be the only act in the circus."

Mr. Pigatto and Mary Ann weren't the only people unhappy with the new schedule. Sam found himself dodging grumpy performers wherever he went that afternoon. There were heated discussions everywhere. No one wanted to give up any time in the spotlight, and Mr. Pigatto was determined to keep the show from running too long.

Even Sam's father was visibly annoyed when he returned to the bus after the Triple Top's evening performance. "Your brother is something else," Sam heard his father whisper to his mother on the other side of the curtain when everyone was in bed. "He stole fifteen minutes from me tonight!"

"He just got a little carried away, Max," Irene soothed. "Besides, the crowd really did like his act. They gave him a standing ovation."

"Sure they did," Max muttered crossly. "Why wouldn't they? He was performing some of my best tricks. That one with the beach towel and the sandcastle? He stole that one from me years ago, when you and I were first dating."

"Well, you know what they say. Imitation is the sincerest form of flattery."

"Humph," Max grumbled. "And another thing; these benches are murder to sleep on. I want my bed back!"

Sam rolled over on his foamie, trying to find a more comfortable position. He sympathized with his father. Sam's narrow bunk wasn't luxurious, but it was ten times better than the floor. When was he going to get his own bed back?

Sam was awake the next morning before dawn. Something soft brushed against him as he sat up, but he couldn't see what it was in the dark. Someone above him was snoring loudly. It sounded like Herbie—or maybe Robbie. Trying not to make any noise, Sam felt his way past the curtain and out the back door of the bus.

His father's voice startled him. "Couldn't sleep either, eh, Sam? Well, pull up a chair."

Sam felt for one of the folding chairs leaning against the bus and set it up beside his father.

"The silence is nice for a change, isn't it?" said Max.

Sam looked up at the stars twinkling peacefully in the sky above him and nodded. "When do we get the bus to ourselves again?"

"When your uncle and his family find somewhere else to stay, I guess."

"But when is that going to be?"

"Patience," said Sam's father. "Believe me, I know how you feel. It's crowded enough in there without Albert and his family on top of us. *Especially* Albert. Your uncle has an ego the size of a small country."

"I really shouldn't have said that," Max said a minute later. "Oh well. I'm sure we'll get through this somehow."

The other occupants of the Stringbini bus got up a few hours later. As he listened to the commotion coming from the kitchen, Sam was grateful he'd snuck a peanut-butter-and-jam sandwich outside.

"Annabel, what's wrong with your face?" Sam heard his mother ask in alarm. "You're all red and puffy!"

Annabel gave a double sneeze in response. "I doh't dow," she wheezed.

"You must be allergic to something," said Irene. "Did someone let one of the animals onto the bus last night?"

"Oliver's still missing," said Robbie.

"I doubt Annabel's allergic to your chameleon,"

said Irene. "Lizards don't have fur or feathers. What about the cats and the magpie? Where are they?"

"Loki's outside, sleeping in his cage," said Harriet.

"The cats are in Mary Ann's bunk," said Martin.

"Snitch!" Sam heard Mary Ann shriek. "I can't believe you just ratted me out!"

"Is that true, Mary Ann?" asked Sam's mother. "Did you smuggle the cats inside?"

"Well, I couldn't leave Cleo and Caesar outside," Mary Ann whined. "They're not alley cats—they're purebred Siamese."

Irene's reply was firm. "No animals on the bus— cats, lizards, birds or otherwise."

A minute later, Mary Ann's precious cats were dumped out the back door of the bus.

"I know just how you feel," Sam said as the two felines stared forlornly at the door. "They kicked me out of my bed too."

Chapter Eight

"Have you seen my juggling plates?" Martin asked Sam half an hour before the show that afternoon. "Louise said she saw you fooling around with them after breakfast."

"I was helping Robbie look for his chameleon," Sam said without looking up from the video game he was playing. "I just moved them aside."

"Well, where'd you put them when you were done?" Martin demanded.

"I didn't put them anywhere," said Sam. "I just looked behind them."

"C'mon, Sammy," said Martin. "I need them for the show. Cough them up."

"I told you. I don't have them, and I don't know where they are."

Martin pulled Sam off the picnic table and put him

in a headlock. "C'mon, tell me where they are. I'm not letting you go until you do."

"What would I want with a bunch of dishes?" Sam said angrily, squirming to break free. He was just about to stomp on Martin's foot when his mother poked her head out of the Stringbini bus.

"Enough already!" said Irene. "If Sam says he didn't take your plates, Martin, he didn't take them. Now let him go."

"He stole them!" said Martin. "Louise saw him!"

"That's *not* what Louise said," said Irene. "Your dishes will turn up somewhere, Martin. In the meantime, you'll just have to improvise."

"Fine, but you aren't playing my *Smash Blasters* anymore," Martin said as he released his brother and grabbed the Pocket-Nitro from Sam's hand. "I'm hiding this where you'll never find it!"

"But I didn't take your stupid plates!" Sam called after Martin's retreating back. "I didn't!"

Sam found his brother's dishes twenty minutes later, when he went back to the bus to get a pile of comics he'd stashed in the cupboard under his bunk. The missing plates were buried under a pile of his jeans and T-shirts.

It took him only a moment to guess who had put them there. It had to be Mary Ann. She'd been furious with Martin for telling his mother about the cats, furious enough to want revenge.

"You didn't have to stick them in *my* cupboard," he muttered as he gathered up the plates and deposited them inside the bunk that temporarily belonged to Mary Ann.

"What are you doing, Sam?"

Sam spun around. Annabel stood in the curtained opening, a look of triumph on her dimpled face. "Wha—what are you doing here?" he asked.

"I lost one of my hair ribbons. I was getting another one."

Sam waved his hands in the air. "It's not what it looks like—"

It was too late. Annabel was already chanting, "I'm telling, I'm telling," as she backed away. The bus door slammed behind her.

Sam plunked himself down beside Harriet in the bleachers a few minutes later. Down below in the center ring, Mr. Pigatto was announcing the first act.

"What's wrong?" asked Harriet.

"She's got me," Sam said miserably. "And I didn't even *do* anything!"

"Who's got you? What are you talking about?"

Sam shook his head. "Don't even ask."

The matinee performance was uneventful right up until the last act. With Annabel's assistance, Magic Max had just performed a series of successful tricks. Now Max was displaying his black top hat. He walked around the center ring and turned the hat upside down to show that it was empty. Annabel stepped forward to join her father in the spotlight. As everyone leaned forward expectantly, Max's young assistant reached into the hat.

Even from his seat high up in the bleachers, Sam could see that something was wrong. There was a bewildered expression on his sister's face, and she had stopped to whisper something into her father's ear.

"What is it?" Harriet asked.

"I don't know," said Sam. "Maybe the hat really is empty. Maybe Snowball is missing."

Magic Max whispered something to his daughter and then signalled for another drum roll. With her eyes screwed shut and her teeth clenched, Annabel reached into the top hat and slowly removed the animal inside.

47

The audience gasped. They'd been expecting a rabbit—not the large lizard that Annabel was holding up in obvious discomfort!

"Oliver!" Harriet and Sam said in unison.

As they watched, Oliver wriggled free of Annabel's grasp and fell to the floor. Annabel squealed and jumped back as the chameleon scurried over her feet and made its escape.

Sam groaned and let his head fall forward into his hands.

"Are you okay?" Harriet asked.

"Just wait—I'm going to get blamed for this too!"

They didn't have to wait long. "I *hate* you, Sam!" Annabel hissed as she stormed onto the Stringbini bus immediately after the show.

Max climbed onto the bus behind his daughter, just in time to prevent her from slugging her brother. "Calm down, Annabel," he said, grabbing both her arms. "As for you, Sam, I think you and I need to take a little walk."

"I can explain," Sam said as soon as they were away from the bus. "I didn't steal Martin's dishes, and I didn't plant the lizard in your hat—"

"Your sister says she saw you put Martin's dishes in Mary Ann's bunk. Is that true?" asked his father.

Sam nodded. "But—"

Max shook his head. "I'm disappointed in you, Sam. First you take your brother's plates, and then you try to frame your cousin."

"I'm the one who was framed!" Sam exploded.

"You don't know for sure that Mary Ann hid those dishes in your drawer," Max said after Sam had finished telling his side of the story. "You should have alerted your brother the instant you found them instead of putting them in her bunk. You know that, Sam."

Sam was silent.

Max ran his fingers through his beard and sighed. "What about the chameleon? What do you know about how Snowball and Oliver got switched this afternoon?"

Sam shook his head angrily. "I told you, I had nothing to do with that. No matter what Annabel says!"

Max studied his son's face. "All right," he said. "I believe you. But I'm telling you the same thing I'm going to tell everyone else. It's hard enough all of us living together without everyone playing pranks on each other. It ends here, are we clear?"

Chapter Nine

The Triple Top caravan arrived on the outskirts of Winnipeg at lunchtime the following Wednesday. Everyone pitched in, and soon the circus was set up for its first performance on Thursday night.

"Hey, wait up," Harriet called as Sam walked toward the main tent with a tray of cotton candy hanging from his neck. "Are you selling that tonight?" she asked.

Sam nodded glumly. "I have to sell snacks at every single performance from now on. It's supposed to keep me out of trouble."

"At least it's something to do. Want some help?" his cousin offered.

Sam shrugged. "Sure. Thanks. Man, it's hot out tonight," he complained as they approached the tent entrance. "They better have the air-conditioning running full blast."

But the temperature inside the tent was even higher

than it was outside. Harriet fanned her face as they stood just inside the entrance. "Whoa—it's like a million degrees in here! Isn't the show supposed to start in fifteen minutes?"

Max was just a few yards away, talking with Mr. Pigatto and the Zuccatos. "What's going on? Why is it so hot in here?" Sam asked his father.

"The generator that powers the air conditioners has died," said Max. "We've called someone to look at it, but who knows when he'll get here. Looks like we're performing in a sauna tonight."

Mrs. Pigatto made her way across the tent toward them. "We're playing to a small crowd," she informed the group as she got closer.

"But the lines outside are huge," said Harriet. "We saw them on our way in."

"Selling tickets isn't the problem tonight," said Mrs. Pigatto. "It's keeping them sold. People step in here and turn right around and ask for their money back. Can't say that I blame them."

Mr. Pigatto wiped the sweat from his brow and shook his head. "We can't afford to cancel. We'll just have to take it easy tonight. And remind everyone to make sure they drink lots of water. We don't want anyone collapsing in the heat."

As the performers dispersed, Sam and Harriet set off to sell cotton candy to the few remaining spectators in the bleachers. "At least no one tried to blame *this* one on me," Sam said to his cousin.

The generator was repaired just in time to cool down the big top for Friday evening's performance. The show was uneventful right until the final act, when Uncle Albert appeared in the center ring. With Mabel's assistance, Albert began the beach towel and sandcastle trick that Max claimed Albert had stolen years before. Albert waved his magic wand and said the magic words, "Salt and sea and air and sand, let a castle appear at my command!"

Mabel dutifully lifted the beach towel to reveal the promised sandcastle. But where the sandcastle should have been—where the sandcastle had been every other time Albert had performed this trick—there was now only a pile of loose sand. Believing it was all part of the act, the audience laughed and clapped dutifully. Then they waited for Albert to finish the illusion.

Sam leaned forward over his tray of cotton candy, curious to see how his uncle would respond. Poor Albert was not handling it well. He was becoming increasingly frantic as he poked the pile of sand with his wand. When the castle still did not appear and the audience began to get restless, Mabel took her husband's arm and tugged him out of the spotlight.

"Man, this isn't going to be good," Sam said as several members of the audience began to boo.

Sam was on his way back to the Stringbini bus when Albert strode past.

"That was a dirty rotten trick you just pulled out there," Albert called ahead to Sam's father, shaking his fist in the air.

Max turned around. "What are you talking about?"

"Don't play innocent with me," said Albert. "I didn't have anything to do with the mix-up in your act last week—you had no right to sabotage mine!"

Max folded his arms across his broad chest. "Calm down, Albert. I had nothing to do with what just happened out there."

"Why should I believe you?" said Albert. "You've been jealous of my act ever since it took third prize in the seventeenth annual Manitoba Magician's Convention."

"Jealous?" Max looked surprised. "My act won a silver medal in the nationals that same year! And even if I *was* competing with you, I certainly wouldn't need to sabotage your act!"

Albert glared at Max for a moment, his hands still clenched. "Yeah, well, you better believe I'll be watching you, Max!"

"Wow," said Sam after his uncle had stormed off. "I was afraid he was going to sock you."

Max took a deep breath before turning to his son. "Tell me honestly, Sam; did you have anything to do with this?"

"No, I didn't," Sam said angrily.

"Are you sure?"

It was Sam's turn to clench his hands. "Of course I'm sure! Why would I do something like that?"

"Maybe to get attention?" Max suggested.

"I don't need that kind of attention," said Sam, shaking his head. "I can't believe this! It's not enough that everyone thinks I'm a loser with no talent. Now I'm getting blamed every time something goes wrong!"

Sam stomped away before his father could say anything more.

Chapter Ten

Sam saw Loki before he saw his cousin. The magpie flew into the grove of trees where Sam was sitting and perched on a branch a few feet above Sam's head.

"Everyone's looking for you," Harriet said as she pushed aside the branches to get to Sam.

"So go tell them you found me," Sam said sullenly.

"I'm not a snitch," said Harriet. "I just thought you might be interested in my notes."

"Notes?"

Harriet fished some loose papers out of the back pocket of her shorts and handed them to Sam. "I've been reviewing everything that's been happening around here lately," she said as she sat down. "All the things that have gone wrong since my family arrived."

"Circus Sabotage," Sam read aloud. "I see you've got my name at the top of the list of possible suspects."

"There have been four incidents since last Sunday," Harriet said, ticking them off with her fingers. "Martin's juggling plates went missing, Snowball and Oliver were switched, the generator for the air conditioners died, and, finally, my father's sandcastle trick was sabotaged. You were sort of involved in the first incident, and circumstantial evidence links you to the animal switch."

"What does that mean—circumstantial evidence?" Sam interrupted.

"It's a technical expression," his cousin explained. "It means that there's no actual proof that you did it, but the evidence seems to point to you."

"Oh, for Pete's sake," said Sam. "I don't have to prove anything to you!"

"Just tell me—did you wreck my dad's trick? I won't tell if you did."

Sam flung his arms out in exasperation. "No, I didn't wreck your father's trick! I didn't do anything to the stupid generator, I didn't plant Oliver in my dad's hat, and I didn't steal Martin's stupid plates!"

"I thought sabotaging a generator was a bit out of your league," Harriet admitted.

Sam grunted. "Thanks, I think. So what about all the other people on your list? You've got my whole family and your whole family down here."

"If it's just one person, it doesn't really make sense, does it?" said Harriet. "Members of both of our families have been targeted. And everyone suffered equally when the air conditioners wouldn't work."

"So who do you think it is, then?" said Sam.

"I don't know. I thought we could keep our eyes open for anything suspicious when we sell cotton candy at the show tomorrow afternoon."

Sam shrugged. "All right. I don't think anything's going to happen, though. Everyone's being too careful."

"Maybe," said Harriet. "I guess we'll see tomorrow."

As usual, the trapeze acts opened the Saturday afternoon show. Herbie and Robbie performed their act first. When the boys were finished, Irene and her daughters climbed the ladder to take their turn in the spotlight. The second trapeze act began smoothly. But just as Elizabeth was turning a double somersault in the air and Louise was preparing to catch her, something small and dark hurtled toward them. Startled, Elizabeth missed her sister's outstretched arms. The audience gasped as Irene, hanging from a second trapeze, swung forward to catch Elizabeth. It wasn't graceful, but Irene managed to grab her daughter by the ankle before she plummeted to the safety net. The crowd cheered in relief.

"That was Loki," Sam said to himself in amazement as he started down the bleacher steps. "What on earth got into him?" With his eyes focused on the bird circling the top of the tent, Sam didn't see the man in the gray suit until it was too late.

"Hey, watch it, kid!" said the man as Sam crashed into his chest.

"Sorry," Sam called over his shoulder.

Harriet ran past just as Sam reached the ground.

"Where did he go?" Sam asked. "I lost him."

Harriet pointed. "Through that gap!"

Sam followed his cousin through a side exit. "Loki, Loki!" they both called once they were outside.

They finally found the magpie in the same grove of trees that had sheltered Sam the evening before.

"Who let you out of your cage?" Harriet asked as the bird flew onto her shoulder.

Loki spread his wings and flapped, then resettled himself.

"Look, he's missing one of his tail feathers," said Sam.

"Someone deliberately hurt him," Harriet said angrily. "He couldn't have gotten out of his cage by himself.

Someone must have taken him out and then yanked out one of his feathers!"

Sam shook his head. "No wonder he was in such a hurry to escape."

That evening, Mary Ann's cats caused a disturbance. As Mr. Pigatto was announcing Mr. Poponopolis and his dog act, the two Siamese cats streaked in through the performers' entrance. They raced into the center ring before anyone could stop them, knocking over the obstacle course that Mr. Poponopolis had just set up and sending the terriers into a frenzy.

As suddenly as they had appeared, the cats were gone. Mr. Poponopolis lunged for his dogs, but they ran after the two cats. Poor Mr. Poponopolis could only stand and shake his fists as the animals disappeared under the bleachers on the far side of the tent.

During Sunday's matinee, Martin opened his unicycle act by juggling a set of dishes. While the dishes spun in his hands, Martin cycled around the center ring. He went faster and faster as the crowd cheered him on.

Without warning, Martin's unicycle suddenly collapsed. Martin was thrown to the ground. The dishes he'd been juggling followed him down, smashing to pieces around him. There were cries of horror from the audience as Irene and Max rushed into the ring.

Sam threw his tray of candy floss aside and raced down the bleacher stairs. He had to elbow his way past a crowd of spectators into the circle of performers that had gathered around his brother. Martin lay groaning on the ground between his parents.

"Is he okay?" Sam asked.

Max nodded curtly. "He's still conscious. Looks like he's going to need stitches, though. And he'll need a doctor to look at his arm."

"I've called an ambulance," a white-faced Mrs. Pigatto said. "It's on its way."

"I'll make an announcement cancelling the rest of the show," said Mr. Pigatto. "We'll need some crowd control too, or the ambulance attendants will never be able to get in here."

"What can I do?" Sam asked his father.

Max shook his head. "Nothing right now. Go back to the bus and wait."

When he returned from the emergency room that night, Martin had a cast on his left arm and twelve stitches in his forehead.

"Are you all right?" Annabel asked tearfully as he limped through the doorway of the bus.

Martin gave his sister a grin. "Hey—it would take more than a little tumble to hurt me."

But Max was not smiling as he followed his son onto the bus. "Dad," Sam began, but his father cut him off with a wave of his hand.

"I have just one thing to say tonight," Max said, addressing everyone on the bus. "I've asked Mr. Pigatto to call a special meeting for the whole circus, nine o'clock sharp tomorrow morning, center ring. And I expect *everyone*," he said, his eyes resting briefly on Sam, "to be there."

Chapter Eleven

Everyone had gathered in the big top by ten to nine the next morning. Mr. Pigatto climbed onto a pedestal and addressed the assembled group.

"I expect you all have a pretty good idea why Max wanted this meeting," he began in an unusually subdued voice. "We've had a number of misadventures recently, and Max and I agreed it was time we all discussed the situation together."

"Let's get right to the point," Sam's father said, stepping up beside the ringmaster. "There's a practical joker among us. Someone who seems to think that endangering members of my family is funny."

"Now hold on a minute, Max," Uncle Albert interrupted. "What about the rest of us?"

"It's not just my family that's been targeted," Max admitted. "But the other pranks were harmless compared to what could have happened to Irene and the twins when that bird flew at them! Not to mention what happened to Martin yesterday. My son's arm is in a cast, and I want to know who's responsible!"

"I think it's Sam," Sam heard Elizabeth whisper to Louise. "He's jealous of the rest of us because he has no talent."

"Ouch!" Sam said angrily as someone poked him in the side. He turned to confront Annabel. "What was that for?"

"I think it's you too," his youngest sister said in a loud voice, putting her hands on her hips. "You knocked over Dad's magic cart on purpose to wreck my disappearing act. I bet you did everything else too!"

"What?" Sam sputtered.

Mr. Pigatto broke in. "That's a very serious accusation, Annabel."

"Well, Annabel did see Sam put Martin's dishes in Mary Ann's bunk," Elizabeth pointed out.

"Yeah," said Annabel. "I saw him!"

Sam's face was burning. "I've already explained that!"

"We need to hear the truth, Sam," his mother said gravely. "Did you loosen Martin's wheel last night? Or play any other pranks on anyone this week?"

"No, I didn't!" Sam said, fighting hard to keep his voice under control.

"Listen, Sam," said Mr. Pigatto. "This isn't a trial. We just need to consider all the possibilities."

Herbie spoke up. "Well, if we're considering *all* the possibilities, Mary Ann has been angry at everyone lately. She keeps talking about revenge."

Mary Ann squealed. "My own brother! I'll get you for that!"

"See?" he said.

Harriet put her hand up. "If you think about it, anyone in our family could have done it."

"What are you talking about?" her father demanded.

"It's just that these 'accidents' didn't start happening until after we arrived," Harriet said.

"But what would your family have to gain from sabotaging the Triple Top?" asked Mrs. Pigatto. "You came here as a last resort."

"Yeah," said Mary Ann. "The truth is the Stringbinis have as much motive to sabotage the circus as anyone in our family."

"Why?" Elizabeth and Louise demanded in unison.

"So you can pin the blame on us and then kick us out," said Mary Ann.

"That's ridiculous!" said Elizabeth.

"We've been totally nice to you!" said Louise.

"Okay, girls," Max said, raising his hands. "You've all made your points. We could come up with a motive for everyone here if we thought about it long enough. Right now we're going in circles. Unless someone steps forward and confesses, we're no further ahead than when we started."

When no one spoke, Mr. Pigatto cleared his throat. "All right, then. Whoever the culprit is, I hope he or she gets the message. We will not tolerate any more pranks in the Triple Top Circus. There will be no more incidents!"

"Thanks," Sam told Harriet as the meeting broke up.

"For what?"

"For standing up for me."

Harriet shrugged. "Think things will get back to normal now?"

"What's normal in a circus?" Sam sighed.

The circus performers remained on alert for the next few days, but as the week passed and nothing happened, they began to let their guard down. By the following Sunday afternoon, they were almost relaxed.

Sam and Harriet were selling cotton candy in the bleachers just before the matinee performance when Sam suddenly elbowed his cousin. "See that guy in the gray suit on the other side? I've seen him before. I crashed into him last week when we were running after Loki."

Harriet squinted in the direction Sam was pointing. "How can you be sure it's the same guy from this far away?"

"It's him for sure. It's not just the suit—he's got a mustache like a walrus."

"C'mon—that's too weird," said Harriet. "We were in Winnipeg last week. He would have had to travel halfway across the province to come to this show."

"So maybe he's a traveling salesman," Sam suggested, "or maybe he's something else."

"Something else," Harriet repeated slowly. "Are you really sure it's the same guy?"

"Positive. Are you thinking what I'm thinking?"

"You mean, do I think he might be the person sabotaging the circus?" Harriet asked.

"Right," said Sam.

Harriet shook her head slowly. "I don't know. Don't you think someone would have noticed him at some point by now, if it was him?"

"Not if he was careful. Maybe he comes at night, when we're all asleep."

"Doesn't the circus have some kind of alarm system?" asked Harriet.

"Not exactly," said Sam. "Mr. Poponopolis's dogs are tied up outside at night. They're supposed to bark and wake everyone up if anyone is sneaking around. But if someone gave them meat or some bones to chew on, they'd keep quiet. It's not like they're real guard dogs."

"I don't know," Harriet repeated. "It could be him, I guess. Let's watch him this afternoon and see what he does."

The show was just beginning as Harriet appeared in the bleachers directly across from Sam. In between his own candy sales, Sam watched the man in the gray suit from his side of the tent. There was definitely something suspicious about him. He didn't laugh or clap with the rest of the audience. He just sat with his arms crossed. As the last act before intermission was starting, he pulled out a cell phone.

A commotion in the center ring interrupted Sam's surveillance. He looked down and saw a trio of clowns buried under a safety net that had somehow fallen on top of them. Other circus performers were already racing into the center ring to help untangle the clowns from the heavy netting.

When Sam looked up again, the man in the gray suit had disappeared. Harriet was also gone. Sam quickly scanned the bleachers on the far side of the tent before hurrying down the stairs toward the nearest exit. Once he was outside, he had to dodge a few mothers and fathers chasing their toddlers. There was no sign of either Harriet or the man in the gray suit until Sam reached the edge of a nearby field that was being used as a parking lot. A dark sedan was just pulling away in a cloud of dust on a gravel road leading away from the field.

"That's him," Harriet announced breathlessly as she appeared at Sam's side. "He got away."

"What happened?" asked Sam. "I looked down when the net fell, and when I looked up again you were both gone."

"He stood up just as the net was falling," said Harriet. "I followed him outside from a safe distance. There was someone in that car waiting for him at the side entrance." She shook her head in frustration. "I tried to get the license plate number, but it was covered in mud. It was a British Columbia plate, though. I could see that much."

"It's got to be him," said Sam. "He's got to be the one sabotaging the Triple Top!"

"Too bad we didn't actually see him *do* anything," said Harriet.

"Oh, come on! Look how he raced away from the scene of the crime!"

"Pretty suspicious, all right," Harriet agreed. "It just doesn't prove anything."

"Yeah, I know—it's circumstantial evidence," said Sam. "But now at least we know who to watch for. I'll be ready for him next time," he promised as he watched the dust on the gravel road settle.

Chapter Twelve

Sam was stacking dismantled circus equipment next to one of the trailers when he overheard his father talking to his mother the next morning.

"We just had a visitor, a Mr. Burkenoff," Max told Irene. "He's a federal safety inspector."

"What did he want?" Sam's mother asked.

"He was here because of what happened yesterday afternoon with the safety net," said Max. "We've just been fined ten thousand dollars for having an 'improperly installed safety device.' If we don't pay the fine in full by the end of the month, Mr. Burkenoff is threatening to shut us down."

"Oh dear," Irene sighed. "This has really gotten serious, hasn't it?"

"Dad," Sam broke in, "I was going to tell you—Harriet and I saw someone yesterday—"

"Hold on a second, Sam," his father said as a black limousine drove toward them. "Looks like we have another visitor."

The limo came to a stop a few yards away. The driver got out first and walked around to open the door for a large, cigar-smoking man.

"Can I help you?" Max asked.

The visitor tapped his cigar with a sausage-shaped finger, and a chunk of ash fell to the ground. "Beaverwick's the name. I heard there was a circus set up out here. Thought I'd drop by and have a look-see."

Max shook his head. "Sorry, I'm afraid you've missed us. We're just packing up."

"Where are you headed next, if you don't mind me asking?" said Mr. Beaverwick.

"All the way to Thunder Bay."

"Fine city, Thunder Bay," said the visitor. "I might be heading there myself on business later this week. Perhaps I'll catch your show there, Mister—?"

"Stringbini, Maxwell Stringbini."

"Ah. The famous magician, Magic Max." Mr. Beaverwick stepped forward to offer his hand. "And this is?" he asked, turning to Sam's mother.

"Irene Stringbini," she said.

"Truth is, Max, Irene, I have a particular interest in circuses." Mr. Beaverwick reached into the breast pocket of his pinstriped suit and withdrew a small card, which he handed to Sam's father.

"Circus Enormicus," Max read out loud. He handed the card to his wife.

"Incorporated, since 1979. I'm the chairman, CEO and majority shareholder," Mr. Beaverwick said as he tapped the ash from his cigar a second time. "Let me fill you in. Circus Enormicus is the largest live-entertainment provider of its kind in the world. Our head office is in Vancouver, but we have shows traveling all over the globe. From Argentina to Zimbabwe, Circus Enormicus is everywhere. We're always looking to sign up new talent."

Irene held out the business card. "Sorry for your trouble, but the Triple Top has always been a small, family-run circus. Max helps manage the business side of things, but each performer owns a share in the show, and that's the way we like it."

"But you could be part of something so much bigger," said Mr. Beaverwick, waving the card away. "Talk it over with the other members of your little group. I'm telling you—Circus Enormicus is the wave of the future."

"We're not interested," Sam's father said firmly, folding his arms across his chest.

Mr. Beaverwick smiled. "Come now. You seem like reasonable people to me. Why don't you just let the idea sit for a few days? If you have any questions, you can call my private number. Anytime, day or night. The number is on the card."

Without waiting for a response, Beaverwick dropped his half-smoked cigar on the dry grass and climbed back into his limo.

"That man spewed more hot air in five minutes than your brother Albert puts out in an hour," Max said to his wife as they watched the limo disappear in a cloud of crickets and prairie dust. "And that's saying something."

Sam's parents seemed to have forgotten that Sam was still waiting a few feet away. "About what I was going to tell you," he started.

"Right," Max said. He checked his watch. "Look, can it wait? We're already running behind, and we've got a few things we need to discuss with Mr. Pigatto before we get on the road."

Sam let out a sigh. "Sure. Whatever."

Later that night as he lay under his blankets on the floor in the sleeping alcove, Sam listened to his parents arguing over Mr. Beaverwick's proposal.

"There's no way the Triple Top is going to sell out to Circus Enormicus," Max insisted.

"Maybe we were too hasty," said Sam's mother. "We haven't even heard Mr. Beaverwick's terms yet."

"Come on, Irene. You've heard the same stories I have. Beaverwick is a tyrant. He has shows touring on six continents, and every single show is exactly the same. He might as well hire a bunch of robots."

Sam heard his mother sigh. "I was there tonight when you went over the Triple Top's finances with Mr. Pigatto. We're in serious trouble, Max."

"I know," said Max. "We were just making ends meet when Albert and his family showed up with six extra mouths to feed. And now we have this morning's fine to pay off on top of everything else."

"Exactly," said Irene. "If things get any worse, we may *have* to consider Beaverwick's proposal."

Chapter Thirteen

"Have you talked to your dad about the man in the gray suit yet?" Harriet asked Sam as they prepared to enter the big top three days later.

Sam shook his head. "Every time I try, he's too busy."

"Maybe it's just as well," Harriet said as she adjusted the straps that held up her tray of cotton candy. "We don't know for sure that he's the one sabotaging the circus. Although I have to admit, he does look kind of familiar."

"Of course he looks familiar," said Sam. "I bet he's been in the audience every time something bad happened."

"He could work for the safety inspector's office," Harriet pointed out. "He could just be watching us for safety violations."

"No, it's him," Sam insisted. "It has to be. We just have to catch him red-handed."

The cousins were making their way slowly up the bleachers when one of their customers called them back.

"What *is* this?" the woman demanded. The two children beside her were gagging and spitting out half-dissolved candy floss.

"Are you trying to poison us?" someone else shouted as more people began to cough and make faces all around them.

"There's something wrong with the cotton candy!" Harriet whispered to Sam, her face white. "What do we do?"

Sam pointed across the tent to the bleachers on the other side. "It's not just us." It was obvious from the noise coming from the other side of the big top that someone had been selling tainted cotton candy there as well.

Mr. Pigatto's voice came over the loudspeaker. "Ladies and gentlemen," the ringmaster began nervously. "I know many of you have already discovered that we've had a PROBLEM with our cotton candy this evening."

There were some angry boos from the audience.

"We do truly APOLOGIZE," the ringmaster continued from the center ring, wiping his rosy face with a handkerchief. "But you'll be happy to hear that we've already identified the problem. It seems that a quantity of ALUM CRYSTALS were somehow introduced into the sacks of sugar that we use to make our cotton candy."

Mr. Pigatto had to shout into the microphone to be heard over the rising noise. "Ammonium alum u.s.p. is a common astringent. It is NOT poisonous. You probably have a bottle in your own medicine cabinets to treat canker sores or sore throats. It tastes absolutely TERRIBLE, but I repeat, alum is NOT poisonous."

The audience was still angry and confused. "So what's this stuff doing in my cotton candy?" one man yelled.

"We are TERRIBLY sorry," said Mr. Pigatto. "I repeat, the cotton candy is not poisonous. It will NOT hurt you. There will be FULL REFUNDS, of course," the ringmaster continued. "And FREE ice-cream bars or caramel corn will be offered to everyone who bought cotton candy this evening."

"Thank goodness it wasn't something poisonous," said Harriet, letting out a ragged breath. "Where are you going?"

"Back to the bus," said Sam. "I'm going to be grounded when my parents catch up with me anyway."

"But you didn't do anything," said Harriet.

Sam looked miserable. "No one's going to believe me this time. I helped make the cotton candy today!"

Sam's father took him aside into the shade of one of the equipment trailers late the next morning. There were dark circles under Max's eyes. "The circus had a few special visitors this morning, Sam. Did you know that?"

Sam shrugged, his arms folded across his chest.

"We had a delegation from the city council of Thunder Bay to start. It seems the mayor and her children were among the people who consumed our tainted cotton candy last night. She wasn't very happy about it, let me tell you."

Sam traced an arc in the dirt with the heel of his sneaker. "I don't know why you're telling me all this. I told you I didn't put anything in the cotton candy."

It was Max's turn to shrug. "I just thought you should know that Thunder Bay has cancelled our permit to perform here this weekend."

Sam looked up in dismay. "That's terrible!"

"That's right," said Max, nodding. "That little prank had some very serious consequences. And it gets worse. The safety inspector, Mr. Burkenoff, showed up right after the delegation from the city. The Triple Top was fined again, this time for violating sections of the health code. That's two fines in less than a week. We have ten days to pay up or we're finished."

Sam's face had clouded over. "But what does all this have to do with me?"

"Nothing, I hope," said Max. "But if there's anything you want to tell me, now would be a good time to get it off your chest."

"I don't have anything on my chest!" Sam shouted. "I've told you that! Why won't you believe me?"

"I don't know what to believe anymore," his father said. "But you have to admit, it doesn't look good that you helped make the cotton candy yesterday."

"Why does it always have to be me?" Sam sputtered. "Why can't someone else be under suspicion for a change?"

Max put his hands up. "Calm down, Sam. Until we figure out who's been pulling these pranks, we're all under suspicion. We can't afford to take any more chances. From now on we're all pairing up. No one can be alone—unless they're using the bathroom.

"It's not just you," Max continued as Sam opened his mouth to protest. "It's everyone. We're all going to be watching each other. Not much fun, but we're running out of other options."

Chapter Fourteen

"Want to be my 'buddy'?" Sam asked Harriet after lunch that afternoon. "I need to get out of here."

Harriet looked up from the book she was reading. "Sure. Are we going anywhere in particular?"

Sam nodded. "The Thunder Bay library. I checked a map; it's only a few kilometers away. You might want to grab those notes you've been taking."

"What do we need my notes for?" Harriet asked as she put a bookmark in her book and stood up.

"I'm tired of being the one everyone points to when something goes wrong," said Sam. "It's time to add someone else's name to your list of suspects."

Harriet raised her eyebrows. "Okay, but what does that have to do with the library?"

"It's just a hunch I have," said Sam. "I need to check something online."

When the cousins reached the library, a young librarian at the circulation desk directed them to the nearest available computer station.

"I've been thinking about the conversation Mr. Beaverwick had with my father," Sam said as he typed Mr. Beaverwick's name into the search engine. "Is it just me, or is the timing of his offer to buy the Triple Top a little suspicious?"

Sam's search word immediately generated hundreds of hits. The first link took them to a recent article from a national newspaper site.

"Wow," said Harriet.

Sam read the article aloud while Harriet took notes. "'Circus Enormicus Incorporated has announced the addition of a new circus to its growing empire. The Leaping Lizard, a familiar name in Canadian entertainment circles since 1929, was recently rescued from bankruptcy by Bartholomew Beaverwick and his associates.' Hey," said Sam, "isn't that your family's old circus?"

Harriet nodded, still scribbling.

"'The Leaping Lizard is the third Canadian circus Mr. Beaverwick has acquired this year,'" Sam continued. "'The previous two circuses were also facing bankruptcy when they were purchased by Circus Enormicus. Mr. Beaverwick has announced his intention to persuade all remaining independent circuses in Canada to join forces under the Circus Enormicus banner."

"I knew the timing of his visit was suspicious!" Sam said excitedly when he was done reading. "Beaverwick *persuades* circuses to join Circus Enormicus by sabotaging them until they're about to go under. Then he makes them an offer they can't refuse. They have no choice!"

"Try that link," Harriet said, pointing to the screen.

Sam clicked on a link that led to an article about one of Circus Enormicus's previous purchases. He let out a whoop when he saw the photograph next to the text.

"Shhh," said the librarian at the circulation desk.

"Sorry," said Sam. His voice dropped to a whisper. "It's the man in the gray suit! The mustache is a little thinner, but it's *him*! I knew it—he must work for Mr. Beaverwick."

Harriet nodded. "You were right! And remember I told you I thought he looked familiar? Now I know where I saw him before. He hadn't grown the mustache yet, but I'm sure he was hanging around the Leaping Lizard just before it went bankrupt."

The photograph the cousins were studying had been taken outside a courthouse in Vancouver. According to the caption under the photo, the owner of the Kit and Kaboodle Circus had taken Circus Enormicus to court to try to stop a forced bankruptcy sale. The photo showed Mr. Beaverwick next to his wife and two of his lawyers. Behind them was a fifth person: the man Sam had bumped into, the man Harriet had followed after the safety net fell on the clowns.

"This photograph proves he's connected to Mr. Beaverwick," Sam whispered. "We've got them both!"

"We haven't actually seen him do anything," Harriet cautioned.

"Look," said Sam. "There's something else."

"What?"

"Look under the photograph. Do you see Mr. Beaverwick's wife's name?"

"Mrs. Audrey Burkenoff-Beaverwick. Nice name. Oh. *Oh!*" Harriet exclaimed, a light going on in her eyes. "Burkenoff!"

Sam nodded. "It all makes sense! Beaverwick must be related to the safety inspector who fined us. We've got to get back to the circus," he said. "We've got to tell my dad!"

"Let me finish my notes," said Harriet. "What am I saying—I'll just print out these pages instead."

As soon as they had paid for the printouts, the cousins hurried out of the library. They ran most of the way back to the Triple Top.

"Where's Dad?" Sam asked Annabel when they reached the Stringbini bus. Annabel was sitting on the grass, playing with paper dolls.

"In a meeting," said Annabel.

"Who with?"

"With Mom and the Pigattos and the men in the long black car," Annabel replied without looking up.

Sam peered around the side of the Stringbini bus. Sure enough, there was Mr. Beaverwick's limousine, half-hidden behind one of the circus trailers. "It's his car all right," Sam said to Harriet. "Mr. Beaverwick must be here right now!"

"Where's the meeting?" Harriet asked Annabel. "In the main tent?"

Annabel nodded. "They won't let you in," she warned. "It's private."

But Sam and Harriet were no longer listening to Annabel. They were already racing to the big top.

Chapter Fifteen

Sam and Harriet entered the tent just as Mr. Beaverwick and two other men in suits were leaving.

"What happened?" Sam asked his parents and the Pigattos when the men were gone. "You didn't sell the Triple Top, did you?"

"Not yet," said Max. "Mr. Beaverwick's lawyers are still drawing up the contract."

"But you *can't* sell out," said Sam.

Mr. Pigatto shook his head sadly. "We don't have a choice, Sam. We can't afford to pay our fines by the deadline. This is the only way to keep the Triple Top from going under."

"But you don't understand," Sam sputtered. "Beaverwick is the one sabotaging the circus!"

"That's quite an accusation!" Sam's mother said. "Do you have any proof?"

Sam and Harriet took turns telling their story, from Sam's first encounter with the man in the gray suit, to what they'd learned from their research at the library.

"Did you ever actually see this man doing anything to sabotage the Triple Top?" Mr. Pigatto asked as he studied the picture Harriet had printed off the Internet.

"No." Harriet shook her head. "But like I said, he was in the audience when Loki flew into the trapezes and when the safety net came down."

"Sorry, guys," said Sam's father. "This is good detective work, but all you've proved is that this man has been in our audience watching us. That might make him a spy on a scouting mission for Circus Enormicus, but it doesn't prove him guilty of sabotage."

"Shouldn't we at least go to the police?" Harriet asked.

"The police would laugh us out of the station," said Mr. Pigatto. "You can't make accusations against someone like Beaverwick without evidence, my dear. Circus Enormicus is an international corporation. We're just a little traveling show—why would they believe us?"

"We can still get evidence," Sam said stubbornly. "It's not too late."

"It *is* too late, Sam," said Max. "He's got us. If we don't come up with the money for our fines by next Monday morning, the Triple Top will be shut down."

"Why can't we come up with the money?" Sam asked. "We have a whole week. Our shows in Hamilton haven't been canceled. That's five performances between now and next Monday."

Mr. Pigatto let his hand fall on Sam's shoulder. "Your father's right, Sam. The fines are just too big. Even if we sold out every performance, we'd still be short several thousand dollars. We've talked to the banks, we've talked to the other performers—we just can't raise enough money. Maybe if we had a little more time…"

"As things stand, we're out of options," said Max. "We have to accept Beaverwick's offer."

"I still can't believe they're letting Beaverwick get away with this," Sam told Harriet two mornings later. The circus was all packed up and on the road again, bound for its engagement in Hamilton. Sam and his cousin had chosen to begin the journey in the back of the Fritzi bus, away from their siblings.

"Does it really matter who owns the Triple Top?" Harriet asked. "You want to leave the circus the first chance you get anyway."

"But it's not fair!" said Sam. "For weeks people have been talking behind my back, saying that I'm the one wrecking things. But now that we know who it really is, no one's doing anything about it!"

Harriet shrugged. "What *can* anyone do? We don't have enough evidence to go to the police. And you heard what Mr. Pigatto said. Even if we sold out every performance between now and next Monday, we still wouldn't have enough to pay off both fines."

"There has to be a way," Sam insisted. "We can't just sit back and let Beaverwick win."

"Are you busy?" Sam asked his parents that evening when the circus convoy was stopped for the night. "Harriet and I were hoping to talk to you about something."

"What's up?" Max asked as they approached a large oak tree where Harriet and the Pigattos were already waiting.

Sam cleared his throat. "We were talking about the fine and how you said we didn't have time to pay it off," he began nervously. "Harriet and I were wondering what would happen if we added extra performances to the schedule this weekend."

"Extra performances?" asked Max.

Harriet nodded. "Like an extra matinee on Friday

for preschoolers and their parents or for school kids on field trips."

"And an extra show on Saturday morning and another one on Sunday evening," said Sam.

Mr. Pigatto rubbed his chin thoughtfully. "That's a very ambitious schedule."

"But wouldn't it be worth it if it meant making enough money to save the Triple Top?" Sam asked anxiously.

"Plus, with my family performing, everyone could take turns," Harriet pointed out. "No one would have to perform in every show."

"Look, it's wonderful that you two want to save the circus," Irene began.

"It's just a real long shot," Max finished for his wife. "To cover our fines, we'd have to sell out every single performance, including the three extra ones you're proposing. We've sold out individual shows before, but never eight in a row. We've never even been close."

"But there are ways we could advertise the circus specially for this weekend," said Sam. "Harriet and I have a whole bunch of ideas."

"Come on, let's hear the kids out," Mrs. Pigatto said. "They've obviously put some effort into this."

"Thank you," Sam said with relief. As the four adults listened attentively, he filled in the details of the plan.

"I have to admit, it sounds intriguing," Max said when Sam was finished.

"It's a long shot, but it just might work," said Mr. Pigatto.

"I don't know about the rest of you," said Mrs. Pigatto, "but I don't want to go down without a fight. I'm in."

"Really?" Sam said in amazement.

"Of course it's not just up to us," Irene cautioned the cousins. "Your plan is going to take a lot of hard work on everyone's part. We'll talk to your brothers and sisters, Sam, but you're going to need everyone else's cooperation too."

"Better get moving," Max said with a smile. "You don't have much time."

The Triple Top caravan pulled into Hamilton late Tuesday afternoon. By the end of the evening, Sam and Harriet had managed to convince even the most reluctant performer to join in the plan to save the circus. While their siblings got ready for bed, the two cousins held a last-minute strategy session at the picnic table outside the Stringbini bus.

"I think that's it," Harriet said a few hours later as she surveyed the scribbled notes and diagrams spread out all around them. "By Thursday night, everyone in the city should know the Triple Top is here."

"Think we can really do this?" Sam asked, suddenly feeling anxious.

"Hope so," said Harriet.

Sam wiped his damp palms on his shorts. "Me too. It would sure be nice to get something right for a change."

Chapter Sixteen

"Uh, thanks for coming, everyone," Sam began nervously, addressing the performers who'd gathered in the big top after breakfast on Wednesday morning. He shuffled the papers in his hands until he found the one he was looking for. "So, uh, we've only got thirty-four hours before the first show on Thursday night. Here's what we thought we should do."

"First, we need to have people patrolling the circus grounds at all times," Harriet said from her place beside her cousin. "We need to make sure there's no more sabotage."

"Absolutely. Good thinking," said Mr. Pigatto as the other performers nodded.

"Everyone else will go into town to promote our weekend shows," Sam said as he and Harriet began handing out the assignments they'd prepared. "As you know, we have to sell out all eight shows or we won't make enough to pay off the fines."

Sam gnawed on the end of his thumb while he waited for the performers to read their handouts. A hush filled the big top as everyone digested the details of the assignments they'd been given.

"Well done, you two," Max said after a moment, looking up from the paper in his hand. "You've laid out our instructions very clearly. Looks like you've thought of everything."

Annabel opened her mouth to say something, but Sam's mother cut her off. "Good job, both of you. Now it's our turn. As Sam said, we don't have much time, so we'd better get moving."

Mr. Pigatto nodded. "You heard the lady. We've got our orders—let's move out!"

While the performers got organized into their assigned teams, Sam and Harriet returned to the Stringbini bus. Sam felt a shiver of anticipation run up his spine as he took his place at the kitchen table. The bus had been converted into a command center. Using borrowed cell phones, the two cousins were set to collect and pass on any information they received.

"Mr. Pigatto just phoned in," Sam informed his cousin a few hours later. "He said the first school show they did went well."

"Good," said Harriet. "Your mother called too. They handed out over a hundred flyers at their elementary school."

"Are they on their way to join up with the others?"

"They're already halfway there," said Harriet.

Harriet and Sam had arranged for everyone to meet for a mini-parade in a busy part of the city at lunchtime. At the stroke of twelve, the Fritzi sisters started the parade on their stallions. As they made their way down the street, the other performers handed out flyers advertising the Triple Top's eight performances that weekend.

When the parade was over, the performers split up into smaller groups again and made their way to the next schools on their lists. When school was out at three o'clock, the groups performed wherever they could find an audience—on street corners, in parks, even in parking lots.

"Everything's going well," Harriet reported to Sam between incoming calls late that afternoon. "Your parents' group has handed out all their flyers."

"Listen to this!" said Sam. "Mr. Pigatto has just been invited to do an interview on one of the local radio stations tomorrow morning!"

"Yes!" said Harriet, pumping her fists in the air. "I don't remember if I told you—my dad called the local newspapers like we asked."

"And?"

"And they promised to send photographers to the parade and to one or two of the school performances." Harriet grinned. "My dad thinks we have a good chance of making tomorrow's front page."

"I can't believe it," Sam said, shaking his head in amazement. "Our plan is actually working."

The performers continued their publicity campaign on Thursday, returning to the circus grounds at four o'clock that afternoon. They checked in with Sam and Harriet before they hurried off to eat and prepare for the first show of the weekend.

"Well?" said Max as he climbed onto the Stringbini bus. "How did it go today?"

Sam let out his breath. "Good—I think."

"We couldn't have done any better with stage one of the plan," said Harriet. "I guess we'll have to wait and see what happens in stage two."

"Good to hear," said Max. He ran the back of his hand across his forehead. "Phew. I'm beat already, and the weekend's just starting. Sure hope all this is worth it."

"Me too," Sam said under his breath when his father was gone again.

Chapter Seventeen

Sam and Harriet went over their checklist one final time, half an hour before Thursday evening's show was scheduled to start.

"The air-conditioning is working?" asked Sam.

"Check," said Harriet.

"Cotton candy's been tested?"

"Check," said Harriet. "And the caramel corn, the snow cones and the hot dogs."

"Ketchup, mustard and relish too?" asked Sam.

"Check, check and check."

"The guards are all in place?"

"Check," said Harriet. "Right now we've got my brothers, the Fritzi sisters, Tina Zuccato and your father on duty. They'll change places with the next shift at intermission."

"And all the cell phones are working?"

"Check. They were all charged overnight."

"No one's called in with anything suspicious yet?" Sam asked.

"Not yet," said Harriet. "Everyone's got a copy of the picture of the man in the gray suit. If anyone sees him or anything strange, they'll let us know right away so we can alert everyone else."

Sam phoned Mrs. Pigatto in the ticket booth. "How are ticket sales?" he asked.

"Fantastic!" said the ringmaster's wife. "We've got extra benches set up inside, but even with the extra seats, we're still going to have to turn people away soon."

"Wait!" Sam said before she could hang up. "Don't let anyone leave until you've sold them tickets for one of tomorrow's performances!"

"Will do," Mrs. Pigatto replied.

"Better get to our own stations," said Harriet. "We've got a whole lot of cotton candy and caramel corn to sell tonight!"

━━━

Sam kept an eye out for the man in the gray suit as he worked the bleachers, but there was no sign of him. When nothing unusual had occurred by the end of intermission, Sam began to relax.

The second half of the evening show also passed without incident. One after another, Sam's friends and family members performed their acts flawlessly, to the delight of the capacity audience. At the end of the night, the tired but happy performers received a standing ovation.

The success of Thursday evening's show was repeated on Friday and again on Saturday. The big top was packed with appreciative spectators for each performance, and each performance ended with a standing ovation.

"If I could have your ATTENTION for a moment," Mr. Pigatto announced in the performers' tent after Saturday evening's show. The room fell silent as the performers all turned to listen to the ringmaster.

"I know you're tired," said Mr. Pigatto. "We've all been working very hard these last few days, thanks to Sam and Harriet's plan. But I think you'll agree that we have a lot to celebrate."

A cheer went up from the assembled group.

Mr. Pigatto beamed. "I would like to propose a toast." He waited while the glasses of punch were distributed. When everyone had been served, Mr. Pigatto raised his glass. "To Sam and Harriet, for coming to the rescue of the Triple Top in our hour of need!"

"Hear, hear," the other performers echoed, raising their glasses.

Sam's cheeks were burning. "Thanks," he said. "But we're not quite done yet."

"We're not?" said his brother Andrew. "But we've already sold most of tomorrow's seats in advance. Doesn't that give us enough money to pay our fines?"

"We can pay the fines this week," said Harriet. "But what about next week or the week after that?"

"What do you mean?" asked Tony Zuccato.

"Well," said Sam, "Mr. Beaverwick doesn't seem like the kind of guy who gives up when he doesn't get what he wants. If he really is behind all of the Triple Top's problems, he's not going to go away just because we beat him this time."

Max nodded. "Sam is right. Beaverwick didn't build his empire by disappearing every time he lost a battle. He's the kind of man who will do whatever it takes to get his way. He'll be back. He'll wait until we have our guard down, and then he'll pounce."

"Oh dear. What can we do?" asked Erma Fritzi, wringing her hands.

"Fortunately, Sam and Harriet have a plan to deal with Beaverwick," Mr. Pigatto replied. "And if it works, we'll never have to worry about Circus Enormicus again."

Chapter Eighteen

"Everything's ready," Harriet told Sam as he joined her at the picnic table outside the Stringbini bus the next morning. "I checked in with Mr. Pigatto. He made the phone calls we asked him to last night."

"Did he specifically mention the fireworks display?"

"He did. He said Mr. Beaverwick sounded interested."

"Good," said Sam. "Now let's just hope that Beaverwick and his friends take the bait."

"How is this plan supposed to work again?" Robbie broke in as he and Herbie hopped off the bus. "We didn't quite get it last night."

"Simple," said Sam. "We're setting a trap. Beaverwick wants to sabotage the circus so he can buy us out, right? So he messes with our fireworks and causes some kind of disturbance that gets us into trouble again."

"Just think what would happen if someone stole

a big firework and lit it inside the big top," said Harriet. "It could set the tent on fire. Or make people panic and start a stampede. Something like that would be the end of the Triple Top."

Herbie looked confused. "We get that you want to catch these guys red-handed. But how are they supposed to steal anything when there are guards watching the fireworks tent around the clock?"

"The guards are going to get called away at the last minute," said Sam. "But we'll still be watching the tent from hiding places nearby."

"R-ight," Robbie said, nodding slowly. "And that's when the bad guys will make their move. Cool!"

"That's the plan, anyway," said Harriet. "And as soon as they leave the tent with the fireworks, we'll jump on them. Then we'll call the police. No one gets hurt and we save the circus."

"Cool," Robbie said again as he and Herbie took off to help Mr. Pigatto move some cases of caramel corn.

Harriet checked her watch and stood up when her brothers were gone. "Time for me to join Mary Ann on guard duty at the fireworks tent. Honestly, I can't believe how cooperative my sister is being all of a sudden."

"Standing up to Beaverwick has made us a team, I guess," said Sam. "Even Annabel is being nice for a change."

Sunday's matinee went off without a hitch. But as the performers came out to take their final bows, there was still no sign of Mr. Beaverwick or any of his associates anywhere on the circus grounds.

Sam called Harriet on his cell phone as the audience filed out of the tent. "You think he's still coming?"

"Of course he is," said Harriet. "We've been counting on him to wait for the last show of the day. He's going to try to send the Triple Top out with a bang, just wait and see."

By seven thirty that evening, everyone was in place and ready for the last performance to begin. At seven thirty-five, Mrs. Pigatto called her husband to let him know that the show was officially sold out.

Sam was standing beside the ringmaster as he took the call. "There are still people lined up out here, and they're not going away," Sam heard Mrs. Pigatto say. "They're setting up lawn chairs and spreading blankets on the ground to wait for the fireworks."

Mr. Pigatto gave Sam a big thumbs-up. "Let's send out a few performers and give them some entertainment while they're waiting," he suggested to his wife.

"That would look good for the TV cameras," Mrs. Pigatto agreed.

"The news crews have arrived, have they?" asked the ringmaster. "I called them, but I wasn't sure they'd be interested."

"Well, apparently they are," said Mrs. Pigatto. "There are no less than three crews out here at the moment."

"Wonderful," said Mr. Pigatto. "I'll check in with you again just before the show."

Harriet called Sam on his cell phone a few minutes later. "He's here! I just saw Mr. Beaverwick's limo pull into the parking lot!"

"Is the man in the gray suit with him?" Sam asked.

"Hang on. No, it's just Beaverwick—and some guy I don't recognize."

"Maybe he's coming separately," said Sam.

"Maybe. So are you in position yet?"

"Just got here," Sam said. "I'm looking through the peephole of the supply tent as we speak. I've got a great view of my dad and Mr. Poponopolis guarding the front of the fireworks tent."

"What about Annabel?" Harriet asked. "Did you check in with her?"

"Yes, she's inside an empty crate behind the fireworks tent, where your dad and Tony Zuccato are on guard duty," said Sam. "I still wish we could have had someone other than Annabel as our lookout."

"Your sister was the only one who would fit in that tiny crate," said Harriet. "It's perfect. No one will ever suspect there's anyone hidden in there spying on them."

"I guess," said Sam. "And we've got lots of other people hiding nearby, ready to jump out as soon as they get the signal." He checked his watch. "It's quarter to eight. Time to call Mr. Pigatto and let him know we're ready for his 'special announcement.'"

"Hey, Sam?" said Harriet.

"Yeah?"

"It's showtime—break a leg!"

Sam grinned. "You too!"

Chapter Nineteen

As Sam peered through the hole in the supply tent, he heard Mr. Pigatto's voice come over the circus loudspeaker. "Attention, this is not a drill. Would all performers please report to the performers' tent for an emergency meeting. I repeat, all performers to the performers' tent."

Sam watched his father and Mr. Poponopolis pretend to argue at the entrance to the fireworks tent. They left a moment later, looking back over their shoulders a few times before they were out of sight.

Sam held his breath as he continued to watch the tent. A minute passed, and then a minute more, but there was no activity. At the five-minute mark, Sam punched Annabel's number into his cell phone.

"Hello?" said Annabel.

"Have you seen anyone yet?" Sam asked.

"Not yet. I'm squished in here!"

"You haven't taken your eyes off the tent, not even for a second, have you?" Sam checked.

"No," said Annabel. "I'm not stupid, you know."

Sam rolled his eyes. "All right," he said. "Don't forget, you have to call Mr. Pigatto the second you see something."

"I know, I know," said Annabel. "Bye."

Sam checked his watch. It was almost eight o'clock. "C'mon," he whispered. "Where are the bad guys? They've got to take the bait!"

The circus loudspeaker crackled to life outside the tent. Sam's heart skipped a beat as he waited for the signal to jump out and help catch the fireworks thief. Instead he heard Mr. Pigatto announce that the evening's show was about to begin.

"No," Sam groaned. "We're running out of time!"

He punched his little sister's number into his phone a second time. "Where are you, Annabel?" he asked when the phone kept ringing. "Pick up!" He hung up and tried again. When Annabel still didn't answer on the third try, he called his dad.

"Sam? Is everything all right?" his father asked.

Sam had already left the supply tent. "It's Annabel," he whispered as he edged around the fireworks tent. "She's not answering her cell. I'm on my way to look for her." He let out a yelp when he spied the open crate a few yards away. "The crate is empty—she's gone!"

"Hang on," said his father. "I'm on my way."

As the news of Annabel's disappearance spread, all the performers who'd been waiting to catch Beaverwick's men came out of hiding.

Tony Zuccato was the first on the scene. "Maybe she left to use the washroom," he suggested.

"Annabel wouldn't abandon her post," said Sam. "Even *she* would know better than that. And look, I found her phone inside the crate!"

Mr. Poponopolis arrived, out of breath. "Any sign of her?"

"Just her cell phone," Tony said as more performers appeared.

"Oh dear," said Erma Fritzi, wringing her hands. "They must have kidnapped her. This is terrible!"

"Hold on," Sam heard his father call behind him. "Look who I found on my way here."

"Annabel!" everyone cried as they turned and saw the little girl holding Max's hand. Sam's sister was crying. Her ringlets were tangled, and there was a grass stain on her knee.

"Oh my goodness. What happened, dear?" asked Erma Fritzi.

"I saw someone sneaking in under the back of the tent," Annabel said through her tears. "A man in a gray suit with a big mustache."

"That's him—Beaverwick's man!" Sam interrupted. "Why didn't you call Mr. Pigatto?"

"I tried!" Annabel sobbed. "But it was dark and I pushed the wrong buttons, and a lady answered."

"There, there," said Erma Fritzi.

"And then the man came out again with a box under his arm," said Annabel. "I got confused, and I couldn't make the phone work. So I followed him. But I tripped, and now I don't know where he went. I'm sorry!" she wailed.

Sam was about to tell Annabel off for letting the bad guy get away, but then he saw the misery in her eyes. She knew she'd let everyone down. Sam knew what that felt like. "It's all right," he said. He gave his sister an awkward pat on the shoulder. "You tried your best."

Max released Annabel's hand. "Do you think you can you find your way back to Mom?"

Annabel wiped her eyes and nodded.

"Good," said Max. "The rest of us need to get moving. We've got to recover those fireworks. If Beaverwick's man tries to sabotage the show, there's no telling what could happen. He could burn the big top down. People could be trampled or burned."

"We've got to tell Mr. Pigatto," said Erma Fritzi. "We've got to stop the show before it's too late!"

"No," said Max, shaking his head. "If we stop the show now, he could set off the fireworks while we're getting the audience out of the big top. People could still get hurt. We have no choice. We have to find him as quickly as possible, before he lights the first fuse."

"Oh dear," said Erma Fritzi. "What if we're too late?"

"That's not an option," said Max. "There are lives at stake!"

Chapter Twenty

The performers split up to search the circus grounds for the man in the gray suit. Sam called Harriet to let her know what was happening.

"Where are you?" he asked.

"I'm in the crowd of people outside waiting for the fireworks to start," she told him. "I'm keeping an eye on Beaverwick. He's giving an interview to a television crew near one of the side entrances of the big top."

"Beaverwick's still here? That's good news," said Sam. "He'll want to be miles away when the first firework goes off. If he's hanging around, it means we still have time."

"He could take off any minute, though," said Harriet. "I'll warn you if he makes a move to leave."

"All right," Sam said. "Talk to you later."

Robbie and Herbie were standing guard just inside the main entrance of the circus.

"Did you hear the news?" Sam asked quietly. "Beaverwick's man stole the fireworks, but he got past us."

The brothers nodded. "Your dad called us," Herbie said. "We're on the lookout."

"You haven't seen anything suspicious yet?" asked Sam.

Sam's cousins exchanged embarrassed glances. "There was a commotion outside a few minutes ago," Robbie admitted. "Some little kid wandered off in the crowd, and the mother was freaking out. We went to help look for him. Someone could have slipped through then."

Sam forced himself to sound calm. "Well, if he did get in, we'll just have to find him."

"Good luck," his cousins called as Sam went into the main tent.

Every face in the audience was turned up. Sam looked toward the roof of the big top and saw his brother Andrew balancing up above on the high wire. He lowered his head again to scan the crowd.

"Any sign of our man?" Harriet phoned to ask.

"Not yet," said Sam. "What about Beaverwick? Is he still out there?"

"He's still here," said Harriet. "Don't worry, I'm not letting him out of my sight."

A sudden motion under the bleachers on the far side of the tent caught Sam's attention. "Hold on a minute. I think I see something."

"What is it?" said Harriet.

"Someone's dragging something behind one of the bleachers. Wait—I think it's just a baby carriage. I'll move in and get a closer look."

Sam edged behind the nearest bleacher and along the outside of the tent. He'd traveled about a third of the way around before he was able to get a good look at the person he was tracking. Sam's heart skipped a beat. It was the man in the gray suit!

"I've found him!" Sam whispered excitedly into his cell phone.

"Be careful, Sam!" Harriet's voice cautioned. "He may be getting ready to make his move. Beaverwick just checked his watch, and he looks like he wants to leave."

"Call my dad," Sam whispered. "Tell him I'm behind one of the bleachers on the north side of the big top. Section P, I think."

"All right," said Harriet. "Keep our suspect in sight, but don't get too close while you're waiting for backup. In the meantime, I'll do my best to keep Beaverwick around."

Sam hid behind the nearest post while he waited for the others. The man in the gray suit was crouched with his back to Sam. As Sam watched anxiously, the man withdrew half a dozen bulky objects from the baby carriage and put them on the ground. Sam gulped as the first firework was unwrapped.

"C'mon, people!" Sam whispered. "Where are you?"

The man selected two fireworks from the pile and carried them both to an open space between two bleachers. No one seemed to notice the man with the fireworks in his hands—the audience was still spellbound by Andrew's performance on the high wire.

Sam couldn't wait any longer. He crept forward on his hands and knees, from post to post. When he was only a few yards away, the man reached into one of his pockets and withdrew a lighter.

"Stop!" Sam yelled as the man lit the first fuse.

The next events were a blur: Tony and Max and half a dozen other performers arrived together, rushing into the space between the bleachers. The man in the gray suit dropped the lit firework and began to sprint away. Sam tripped as he was chasing him and fell against Mr. Poponopolis. Mr. Poponopolis knocked over Max, who fell on top of Robbie, who in turn tripped Tony. Tony landed on top of several people, including the man who was trying to get away.

As they lay sprawled on the ground, Harriet suddenly appeared, dragging Mr. Beaverwick with one arm and a television reporter with the other. "See?" Sam heard his cousin say. "I just *knew* you'd want to see this firsthand. What goes on behind the scenes of a circus is even more interesting than what happens in the center ring!"

In the first few seconds of chaos, the lit firework was temporarily forgotten. The flame had burned its way through most of the fuse when Sam heard his father yell, "Everybody get down!"

There were some shrieks from above as several people lunged for the lit firework at the same time.

"It's going to go off!" someone screamed as the flame traveled down the last few inches of the fuse.

Just then, something dark hurtled past them through the air.

"Loki!" Harriet shouted.

The magpie grabbed the lit firework in its claws and flew swiftly toward a gap in the tent wall. The bird had just cleared the gap when a tremendous boom shook the tent.

"No," Harriet sobbed, lifting her hands to her mouth in horror. "Loki! Come back!"

As requested by Sam and Harriet, Mr. Pigatto had sent free invitations to several police officers and their families for Sunday evening's performance. The officers made their way to the scene of the commotion immediately. With eyewitnesses all around, it didn't take them long to sort things out. Once the man in the gray suit was safely in custody and the remaining fireworks were accounted for, Harriet presented the police with a copy of the photograph linking the man to Mr. Beaverwick. She and Sam took turns describing how the circus had been repeatedly sabotaged.

"He's trying to get away!" Annabel exclaimed suddenly. She pointed toward Mr. Beaverwick, who was making for one of the side exits. The circus tycoon didn't get far. Martin stuck his leg out to trip him, and Herbie and Robbie leapt on top of him.

"Any statement for the press, Mr. Beaverwick?" a television reporter asked as the owner of Circus Enormicus was led away for questioning.

"Get that microphone out of my face!" Mr. Beaverwick thundered. "I'm not talking until I see my lawyer!"

Mr. Pigatto had to shout into his own microphone several times before he could reclaim the audience's attention. "LADIES and GENTLEMEN! We APOLOGIZE for the disturbance. We're going to take a brief intermission to give the police officers time to wrap up their investigation. We'll be back as SOON as we can with the second half of our show. And be sure to stay around afterward for our FIREWORKS DISPLAY. We promise it will be well worth the wait!"

"We did it!" Sam crowed to Harriet when he finally found her in the crowd of people jammed in around them. "We saved the Triple Top!"

"But I lost Loki," said Harriet. There were tears streaming down her face.

Sam lifted his hand to pat his cousin's shoulder, and then he caught sight of something that made him smile. "Look over there!"

Harriet turned in the direction Sam was pointing. Mrs. Pigatto had just entered the big top through the performers' entrance, with a slightly ruffled-looking black and white bird perched on her shoulder. "Loki!" Harriet cried, her hands flying to her mouth. "But how—?"

"He must have dropped the firework just before it went off," said Sam. "That's one smart bird!"

"Happy endings all around," said Max, who'd come to stand beside his son. "Well done, you two! Well done!"

Chapter Twenty-one

It took the circus performers several days to recover from the excitement of the weekend's events. Just when it seemed that things were returning to normal, Uncle Albert asked Mr. Pigatto to call a meeting in the center ring.

"Well, my friends," Albert began, "I can't begin to thank you enough for the hospitality you've shown my family. It's been quite an adventure."

There were some laughs and groans from the other performers.

"Still," Albert continued, "I know it's been a strain squeezing another family into the circus, not to mention the Stringbini bus."

"It's been a bit of an adjustment," Max admitted with a smile. "But we've managed."

Albert tipped his head at his brother-in-law. "Thank you, Max. You've been more than generous, but I have good news. With Beaverwick and his men facing charges, the Leaping Lizard was put back up for sale. The previous owners have raised enough money to buy it back, and they've asked us to return."

"That's wonderful news for you, Albert," Mrs. Pigatto beamed.

"But sad news for us, of course." Max spoke sincerely. "I was just starting to get used to the extra company. You'll be missed around here."

The others nodded, murmuring their agreement.

Sam alone remained silent. He felt all his recent happiness escaping, like air from a deflating balloon. Just when life in the circus had finally become bearable, Harriet was going away.

Max cleared his throat. "The Goldfingers and the Stringbinis have one more announcement to make. But first, I know you'll all agree when I say that we owe Sam and Harriet a huge thank-you for coming up with a plan to save the Triple Top. Beaverwick met his match when he took you two on!"

Sam felt his cheeks flush as the performers cheered. "Way to go—well done!"

Max waited for the applause to die down before continuing. "I think a few of us also owe Sam an apology for the accusations we made against him."

"I'm sorry," Annabel mumbled as her mother nudged her forward.

"Me too," said Louise.

"Me too," said Elizabeth.

Max put his hand on Sam's shoulder. "And I'm sorry for ever doubting you, Sam. You swore you were innocent, and that should have been enough."

"It's all right," Sam said, staring intently at his sneakers.

"Good," said Max. "And now for our announcement. We've been talking, and we've agreed that it isn't fair to continue dragging Sam and Harriet from town to town. They're both bright kids with bright futures, but their futures aren't in the circus." Max turned to face the two puzzled cousins. "If you're interested, we're willing to enrol you at St. Michael's Academy in Ottawa. It's one of the best schools in the country. You can stay with your Aunt Katrina."

"My sister Katrina left the circus years ago to become a dentist," Irene explained to the group. "Her kids are grown up and her husband died a while back. She still lives in Ottawa, though, just a stone's throw away from St. Michael's. Remember her big house, Sam? We spent Christmas with Katrina a few years ago. What do you say, you two?"

It took Sam a moment to find his voice. "Both of us? We could both go?"

"What about Loki?" Harriet asked.

"Katrina has invited Loki too," said Irene. "You know how she loves animals."

Martin punched his brother lightly on the arm. "I'd take the offer and run if I were you, Sammy."

"But what about you guys?" Sam asked, feeling a lump form in his throat at the thought of leaving his family.

"Oh, I think we'll manage to hold down the fort somehow," Irene said.

"And you won't be away from us forever," Max assured him. "We'll call you at least once a week, and you can catch up with us on the road at the beginning of every holiday. Thanksgiving, Christmas, Easter, summer vacation—you'll be so sick of us, you'll be counting down the days until you're back in Ottawa."

"Well?" asked Uncle Albert. "What do you think?"

Sam looked over at Harriet. Her eyes were suspiciously shiny, but she was smiling and nodding her head.

"Well," Sam said, taking a deep breath, "I guess I could give it a try. When do we leave?"

Rachel Dunstan Muller was born in California and immigrated to Canada when she was two. With the exception of a year in Northern Ireland, she has lived on the west coast of British Columbia since childhood. Rachel has been an English tutor, a ferry worker, a newspaper columnist and a training consultant, but writing fiction is her favorite occupation. Her first book with Orca was *When the Curtain Rises*. She currently lives on the edge of a small Vancouver Island community with her husband, four daughters, and an ever-changing assortment of cats, rabbits, birds, rodents, amphibians and fish.